SPIRITUALITY OF
INTERFAITH DIALOGUE

A Call to Live Together

SPIRITUALITY OF INTERFAITH DIALOGUE

A Call to Live Together

Editors

Ambrogio Bongiovanni

Leonard Fernando

2019

Spirituality of Interfaith Dialogue: *A Call to Live Together* – Published by the Rev. Dr. Ashish Amos of the Indian Society for Promoting Christian Knowledge (ISPCK), Post Box 1585, Kashmere Gate, Delhi-110006.

ISBN: 978-93-88945-41-7

Cover Picture Reference:

Jesus washing the feet to his disciples *(from the Gospel of John 13: 1-20)*

Sculpture at Tulana Research Centre for Encounter and Dialogue Kelaniya - SRI LANKA.

Artist: Ven. Uttarananda Thera: Painter, poet, writer, sculptor, and founder of the Humanist Association of Bhikkhus, Ven. Uttarananda studied at the Brera Academy in Milan. While in Italy, he lived for a short time in a Benedictine monastery, a sojourn he recalls as a profoundly moving experience.

Laser typeset by

ISPCK, Post Box 1585, 1654, Madarsa Road, Kashmere Gate, Delhi-110006 • *Tel:* 23866323

e-mail: ashish@ispck.org.in • ella@ispck.org.in
website: www.ispck.org.in

Dedicated

To the victims of
violence and religious intolerance in the world.

Contents

Preface

by Meir M. Bar-Asher
The Hebrew University of Jerusalem

The idea that interreligious dialogue in today's world is essential rather than optional is universally recognized by clerics and laity alike. From the time of the Second Vatican Council (1962-1965) efforts have been made by the Catholic Church to allay tensions between religions and create an atmosphere of dialogue and understanding. The most prominent expression of this endeavour is the celebrated document *Nostra Aetate* ("In our time"), published by the Vatican on October 28, 1965. This document, promulgated by Pope Paul VI, constitutes a "declaration on the relation of the Church to non-Christian religions".

The opening paragraph states: "One is the community of all peoples, one their origin, for God made the whole human race to live over the face of the earth. One also is their final goal, God. His providence, His manifestations of goodness, His saving design extend to all men, until that time when the elect will be united in the Holy City, the city ablaze with the glory of God, where the nations will walk in His light."

Nostra Aetate opened a new era in the attitude of Christianity towards other religions. The document was aimed first and foremost at the rival sister-religions, Judaism and Islam, but also at other faiths. It is well known that the relations between the three Abrahamic religions have been characterized by unceasing, violent struggle both on the level of virulent polemical writings and in bloody conflict, which each side viewed as "holy wars". Violence of this kind has tended to characterize relations between the other religions too. In light of this state of affairs, the *Nostra Aetate* declaration can be viewed as a turning-point in the history of interreligious relations. Joseph Satyanand, a leading expert in the field of Hindu-Christian dialogue and one of the contributors to the present volume, pertinently defined the document as the "Magna Carta of Interreligious Dialogue". He goes on to use another powerful image, stating that the document "marked a 'Copernican revolution' in the attitude of the Church towards world religions by opening her doors wide for dialogue and cooperation with all people of good will by removing misunderstanding, prejudices and elements of hatred"

It is worth noting that a growing awareness of the importance of interfaith dialogue exists outside the Church too. Prominent non-Christian religious leaders around the world have readily adopted this line of thinking. On various occasions the 14th Dalai Lama has declared that "the 21st century is the century of dialogue and interreligious dialogue is the key to ending violence and terrorism in this world". A similar approach is reflected in the "Document of Human Fraternity" (Documento sulla Fratellanza Umana), which was signed by Pope Francis and Dr Ahmad al-Tayyib, rector of the al-Azhar Mosque in Cairo – the most significant religious institute in the Sunni Muslim world – in Abu Dabi on February 4, 2019. This document, which was recently discussed in depth in a colloquium held in the Jesuit Faculty of Theology San Luigi in Naples (June 20-21, 2019) in the presence of Pope Francis, constitutes a substantial continuation of the *Nostra Aetate* declaration. It is the culmination of an extended dialogue between the two great religious leaders. Its stated aim is to invite "all persons who have faith in God and faith in human fraternity to unite and work together so that it may serve as a guide for future generations to advance a culture of mutual respect in the awareness of the great divine grace that makes all human beings brothers and sisters."

The great significance of the present work, admirably edited by Ambrogio Bongiovanni and Leonard Fernando, is the broadening of the scope of the religions under discussion. In addition to the three Abrahamic faiths, which do not lack coverage in contemporary discourse, the book offers a superb variety of chapters pertaining to East Asian religions, mainly Hinduism and Buddhism, which are thoroughly examined from the perspective of their approaches to interreligious dialogue.

In almost every religion it is easy to find texts that confirm a tendency to reject dialogue with the other and impose notions of exclusivism. Throughout history this approach has produced extensive polemical literature aimed at denigrating and delegitimizing the other. Needless to say, such an attitude has generated neither peace in the world nor mutual respect between religions and cultures. For the authors participating in the present work it is vital to counter this with efforts in the opposite direction – namely, to point to the positive trends in interreligious relations.

The axis around which all the chapters of the book revolve is the distinction "between the spirituality of dialogue and the dialogue of spirituality". In his own contribution, entitled "Mercy: A Key-category for the Spirituality of Dialogue", Bongiovanni refers to this distinction: "Spirituality is indeed the driving force that encourages the participants of our encounters and seminars that have been conducted in India and Italy for the last twenty years, by means of a partnership of organizations, especially the support and encouragement of *Movimento S. Francesco Saverio*, and individuals: scholars, teachers, students and social activists".

The authors develop the dialogical line of thinking, each in his or her own direction, with the common denominator – reflected in most chapter titles – of pursuing the *spirituality of dialogue*. In other words, a prerequisite for devoting oneself to interreligious dialogue is the presence, in oneself, of a spirit of dialogue. Only when such a spirit exists can one begin to consider the spiritual (and even non-spiritual) contents of the dialogue.

Each of the book's chapters contributes significantly to the rich and complex delineation of the subject in question. Of necessity, I will limit myself here to a general outline. The editors finely considered introduction is followed by eight chapters. The first, by M. Paul Raj, presents an extensive and in-depth study of the dialogical elements of the Old and New Testaments of the Bible. He shows that this voice, which is usually overlooked by scholars and readers of the Bible, is a key element in the preaching of the prophets of Israel and that of Jesus and some of his Apostles. Subsequent chapters demonstrate the centrality of dialogical thought in both Christianity and Islam (Chapters IV and VII, by Shaheena Khatib and Anad Mathew, respectively, focus on Islam).

Eastern religions, notably Hinduism and Buddhism, are also well represented in a number of chapters. Chapter III (by Anil D'Almeida) instructively considers the phenomenon of Hindu pilgrimage as a space in which religious proximity, partnership and even dialogue are created. Hinduism is discussed in connection with Christianity in the above-mentioned Chapter VI (by Joseph Satyanand), yielding some fascinating insights. Chapter V (by Dechen Dorjee) offers valuable observations, such as the importance of distinguishing between "tolerance" and "dialogue". The former by no means implies the latter, since tolerance towards the other may be accompanied by complete indifference and unwillingness to discuss his beliefs. The author also rightly raises the question of reluctance to engage in dialogue out of fear that the other's faith may affect his own beliefs: "We also have to challenge the sense of superiority or inferiority of one faith over the other, or one community over the other, so that we meet each other on a level playing field. Meeting this way doesn't mean that we have to forget our differences and assimilate". The final chapter (by Jerome Sylvester) is dedicated to religious cosmopolitanism, exploring an important dimension that has been largely neglected by scholars of interreligious dialogue.

It is important to emphasize that the strong dialogical approach found in this impressive collection of essays is far from being the outcome of a naive reading of the history of the various faiths or of any lack of awareness as to the violence that has stained their respective histories. Rather, it emerges from a powerful desire to open new horizons towards a better future for the entire world. We are urged to direct our gaze towards those aspects of religion that call for affection towards the other, a respect for his beliefs, doctrines and rites, and a quest to build bridges between religions rather than walls and barriers. In the words of the aforementioned document signed by Pope Francis and the rector of al-Azhar, the role and ambition of humanity should be to "never incite war, hateful attitudes, hostility and extremism, nor must they incite violence or the shedding of blood [...] and to stop using religions to incite hatred, violence, extremism and blind fanaticism, and to refrain from using the name of God to justify acts of murder, exile, terrorism and oppression".

The well-judged addition of three appendices lends further weight to the book's contents: (a) *Nostra Aetate* ("In our time"): Declaration on the Relation of the Church to Non-Christian Religions, proclaimed by his Holiness Pope Paul VI on October 28, 1965; (b) the letter to Presidents of Bishops' Conferences on the Spirituality of Dialogue issued by the Pontifical Council for Interreligious Dialogue; and (c) the address by His Holiness Pope John Paul II to participants in the plenary assembly of the Pontifical Council for Interreligious Dialogue (1995).

In summary, this book makes a vital contribution to the field of interfaith discourse, exploring fundamental concepts and examining the religious views of the major religions in the contemporary world. The book also makes it clear that interfaith dialogue does not require its participants to compromise or give up their religious identity. On the contrary, their spirituality may be enriched by the dialogue experience. Just as the beauty of a rainbow depends on each one of its constituent hues, so every religion on earth has its distinctive place in the overarching spirituality of mankind.

Introduction

Interreligious dialogue is a gift of the second session of the Second Vatican Council. The Declaration, *Nostra Aetate,* opened a new vista for the mission of the Catholic Church towards the people of other religions. It is recognized, therefore, as a milestone in the history of dialogue not only by Christians but also by many believers of other religious traditions. In fact, the aim of the document was to help the Christian community change its perception of the 'other' and promote unity and love among people of different faith traditions and nations.

> «One is the community of all peoples, one their origin, for God made the whole human race to live over the face of the earth. One also is their final goal, God. His providence, His manifestations of goodness, His saving design extend to all men, until that time when the elect will be united in the Holy City, the city ablaze with the glory of God, where the nations will walk in His light».[1]

Soon after the celebration of the Golden Jubilee year of that document, a seminar on the 'Spirituality of Dialogue' was held in August 2016 in Varanasi India, one of the holiest places for Asian religions. The seminar was timely and relevant and very useful. It had not merely theoretical discussions on spirituality but it was indeed a call to live together in dialogue, sharing the richness and the goodness of one's own religious experience. In many ways it was a reminder of *Nostra Aetate* and a tribute to its spirit.

This book offers the readers the most relevant reflections and the main topics presented during the seminar from Christian, Muslim, Hindu and Buddhist perspectives, with the hope that this will encourage both new and meaningful encounters among people of good will in all religious traditions in their search for God and an interfaith spirituality. We hope that this endeavour will be appreciated from both the spiritual and intellectual points of view.

The author of the first chapter, Dr. Paul Raj, SJ, a professor of Sacred Scripture, explores in the Christian Scriptures how dialogue can be made possible in the multi-religious context of India. He presents quotations that would motivate Christians to enter into dialogue with other religions.

Dr. Ambrogio Bongiovanni, who inspired the theme of the seminar, brings up the call for works of mercy, envisaged by Pope Francis for the Extraordinary Jubilee of Mercy. He shows the difference between spirituality of dialogue and dialogue of spirituality, and, through some biblical references, presents God's mercy as a key-category for the spirituality of dialogue in the current time.

Dr. Anil D'Almeida, SJ presents the theme of pilgrimage and devotion in popular religion in the Indian context. The pilgrim's spirituality, which is a never-ending approach to God even in a secularized and technological post-modern age, is a transforming spirituality; it is always dynamic and interactive, and no one will be left untouched by it. This work would motivate people to engage in academic research to re-visit and re-interpret the role of popular religiosity.

Four chapters are focused on the contribution from different religious worldviews: Islam, Buddhism and Hinduism.

A Muslim woman scholar, Dr. Shaheena Khatib, in her brief but well articulated paper introduces to us the spirituality of dialogue and social harmony through some selected readings of the Qur'ān.

Dr. Dechen Dorjee, a Buddhist monk and scholar, points out his perspective on the Buddhist efforts in understanding religious pluralism by the promotion of dialogue and social involvement of Buddhism, overcoming the general idea of tolerance and the complex of superiority/inferiority towards the other.

A chapter on the Hindu and Christian approach to the spirituality of dialogue forms the next section of this book. Dr. Satyanand IMS, a catholic priest specialized in Indology and in the study of Hindu Scriptures, shares his expertise and experience of the Hindu-Christian dialogue. It is interesting to note the way he brings out persuasive comparisons from the scriptures that would compel the dialogue-partners to follow his steps.

Dr. Anand Mathew, IMS works with the Muslim community and is actively engaged in dialogue on right-based issues for social transformation through low cost media, such as street theatre and media campaigns. His long association with the Muslims for social unity (*Quamiektha*) has set the tone of his presentation from the background of communal violence and religious conflicts. Being an activist for peace and harmony he shares his experience and reflection on these issues and how he developed a spirituality to cope the situations of conflicts.

Finally, Dr Jerome Sylvester, IMS almost sets tone to a new discussion from the point of 'Religious Cosmopolitanism' as spirituality of dialogue in the third millennium. His argument is based on the experience of the Asian 'triple dialogue' and the religious experience of those who believe in Christ, known as *Khristbhaktas*. The concept of religious cosmopolitanism invites all religions into partnership for dialogue and to collaborate in the action for social transformation.

The book concludes with three appendixes: the Declaration of the Second Vatican Council *Nostra Aetate* and two important contributions on the theme of the Spirituality of Dialogue dating back two decades which Bongiovanni recalled in his chapter, namely the Address of John Paull II to the participants in the Plenary Assembly of the Pontifical Council for Interreligious Dialogue (1995) and the Letter of Card. Arinze, President of the Pontifical Council for Interreligious Dialogue (PCID) on the Spirituality of Dialogue to the Presidents of Bishops' Conferences (1999). That is not only a remembrance of the sensibility on the themes of John Paul II and of PCID, but also a good wish to continue that reflection at Official level.

Several participants enriched the Seminar with discussion, questions and prayers, contributing to its success and, not least, creating an atmosphere of friendship and fraternity: members of the Maitreya Xavier Charitable Society with their President Mr. Anthony Cruz, students of the Theological College of the Indian Missionary Society in Varanasi who attended some lectures and animated the prayer meetings, the then Principal of Vidyajyoti College of Theology Fr. Dr. Leonard Fernando SJ, Dr. Reeta Bagchi a Hindu scholar, professor of Comparative religious studies at Hamdard University in Delhi and Dr. Maria Teresa Mercinelli from Italy.

Not least, it is worth recalling a few who other people who contributed to the success of the Seminar. Fr. Savari Raj, the then Director of Chetanalaya Centre of the Catholic Archdiocese of Delhi, offered to the participants the experience of the Centre: "building people an instrument of dialogue for attaining new and just social order". Such an experience is perhaps a concrete example of implementation of one aspect of the "triple dialogue" encouraged by FABC, Federation of Asian Bishops' Conferences: building up Basic Human Communities where dialogue becomes the unifying factor to meet the challenges of plural societies.

Dr. Mohammad Arif shows the long history of the dialogical encounter between Islam and Hinduism and the influences that both religions received from each other in the Indian context, notwithstanding the communal tensions which cast a deep shadow on the relationship between people of various religions.

Rajeshsri Gange Hans, a Hindu scholar, Dr. Nirmal Jain, Mr. Dharveer Singh a Sikh Guru, spoke in one voice for the need to collaborate with one another in establishing social harmony and peace as prerequisites for real development and stability of the human community.

We express a sense of gratitude to Movimento S. Francesco Saverio in Italy for the financial and spiritual support for the project; to Fr. Jerome Sylvester of the Indian Missionary Society, for his precious cooperation, support and advice in the organization of the Seminar and the exposure programme; to Dr. Atola Longkumer for her qualified proofreading service and suggestions during the editing; finally, to Mr. Anthony Cruz, Mrs. and Mr. Toppo, Mr. Amit Jalbandha of Maitreya

Xavier Charitable Society for their valuable contribution to the organization of the Seminar.

Ambrogio Bongiovanni
Leonard Fernando
The Editors

"God desires everyone to be saved and to come to the knowledge of the truth" (1 Tim 2:4)

Biblical Foundations for a Spirituality of Inter-Faith Dialogue

M. Paul Raj SJ

In every multi-religious context similar to the one found in India, developing a 'theology of religions' is a must, because the God believed in and spoken of in every religion has to be one and consequently the truth-claims made by every religion must somehow relate to this one and the same divinity. Such a 'theology of religions' necessarily calls for more than anything else a dialogue between the different religions and would seriously take into consideration the different elements such as services, rituals, stories, doctrines, beliefs, communities, architecture and music of every religion, and most importantly it has to relate the different 'experiences' of God on which the different religions are founded. Such a 'God-Experience' is contained and expressed in the foundational texts of every religion and it makes it imperative to seriously look into those texts in order to find out if a particular religion is capable of

an authentic dialogue. In this short essay an attempt is made
to consider the 'dialogue-friendliness' of the Bible.

Dialogue as Sharing of Experience

Every inter-religious dialogue, in which people of different
religions come together not merely to share their ideas but
their experiences which are foundational for their faith and
praxis, should be governed by the principles of sensitivity,
cautiousness, mutual openness and respect. While there is the
possibility of exaggerating one's attachment to one's religion
from a fundamentalist point of view, still even an authentic,
moderate attachment is capable of preventing a person from
being open to other religious traditions. Belongingness to a
religion,[1] which binds all its members together on the basis of
a specific God-Experience, is comparable to the *umbilical cord*
relationship between mother and child and is deeply personal
and strongly emotional providing its members security and
identity. That is why one must be extremely sensitive to the
emotional aspects of every religion when one gets involved
in any kind of inter-religious attempt, be it an interreligious
liturgical celebration, or an intellectual dialogue or a liberative
and emancipatory praxis. One must refrain from making attempts
to present one religion as superior or better. Such efforts would
amount to raising meaningless questions like, 'who is the best
mother in the world?' One may attempt to describe the qualities
of different mothers, but ultimately, almost every human being
would conclude saying: 'My mother is the best!'

Yet not all the mothers exercise their motherhood in the
same way. Further, every human mother could also have her
own strengths and weaknesses. So, when mothers come in
contact with one another, then they can either learn ways and

means of overcoming one's weakness or even if one does not lack in anything, still everyone can discover 'other' ways of fulfilling one's duties as a mother. So also, in every inter-faith dialogue the members of different faiths can 'learn' from the members of another religion.

Inter-faith dialogue as sharing of the core experience also implies certain amount of 'religious tolerance.' This does not mean accepting the *content* of the beliefs and actions of other religious people,[2] which would result in some kind of syncretism, but involves accepting *someone* who is holding such beliefs and models one's life on the basis of these beliefs.[3] Religious tolerance means that people of different religions live 'in harmony' with one another without falling victims to prejudice, condemnation and self-righteousness allowing a sense of mystery to exist in what each one is and believes. It would enable every religious person to remain God-centred and not institution-centred. The same is true also of dialogue with an addition that an inter-religious dialogue also attempts at understanding the 'commonalities' in the content of different religions.

The Church documents also insist on the necessity of dialogue with other religions. The document *Dominus Jesus* which does not appear to be very dialogue-friendly, still makes it clear that inter-religious dialogue requires an attitude of understanding and a relationship of mutual knowledge and reciprocal enrichment, in obedience to the truth and with respect for freedom.[4] Long before this document, the Vatican Secretariat for Non-Christian Religions has already in 1984 affirmed that "any sense of mission not permeated by such a dialogical spirit would go against the demands of true humanity and the teachings of the gospel."[5] The encyclical Letter of John Paul

II, *Redemptoris Missio,* also affirms in its paragraph 55 that dialogue and mission cannot be separated though it perceives dialogue only as a strategy to subduing other religions.

The Indian Christian Context

The Church in India is involved in a large network of educational, health and social service institutions which enables a harmonious living with the other religious people.[6] Yet there is a conflict in the Church of India between such a universalist praxis and exclusivist theology.[7] The 'ray of truth' theology of the Second Vatican Council has not yet been transcended. Probably such a theology is the outcome of the exclusivist historical contexts of the earlier centuries in which Christianity had to survive and of the powerful and sometimes even aggressive missionary strategies of the past, especially during the Middle Ages. A combination of exclusivist approach and powerful missionary strategies can never be the best pre-conditions for a dialogue with other religions. That in no way prevents us from studying the dialogue-friendliness of the Bible.

Is the Bible Dialogue-Friendly?

At the outset it must be clear to the readers that the Bible does not contain "any comprehensive solution" to the contemporary challenge faced by the Church in terms of Christianity's relationship with other religions.[8] It is generally presumed that the Bible is not at all interested in such a dialogue. However, I think it is not all that obvious what the Bible has to say on this theme. Yet, I am convinced it has a lot to say about how one should approach the people of other faiths. In order to understand the biblical texts which directly or indirectly address the relationship between people of different religions, one should keep the following in mind.

Firstly, it should be noted that the Bible is the 'word of God' in the 'words of the human beings.' It implies that the Bible has been composed by creative human authors and they have written down the message of God to the human beings which he chose to reveal to them. Thus, what is found in the Bible contains divine interventions in human / cosmic life and human appropriations of the same. And one could identify a world of differences between the two. That is why throughout the Bible, the LORD struggles to communicate with the humans who do not exactly understand what the Lord communicates to them and even in case they understood they do not agree with him and even when they agreed with him they fail to convert it into praxis.

The later readers of the Bible in the last twenty and odd centuries have also interpreted or misinterpreted the biblical texts from each one's vantage point of view. Here the historical and cultural distance between the biblical texts and the 'language' used cause further difficulties. The historical and cultural gap is reduced if not totally bridged by accessing the historical critical methods which are officially used also in the Catholic exegesis since 1943 thanks to the document *Divino Afflante Spiritu* of Pope Pius XIII and one is able to arrive reasonably at the original intentions of the text or the author. However, the problematic of language as a neutral medium communicating objective truths remains. By implication when we read the biblical texts today, we have to be extremely careful not to fall prey to any kind of extra-contextual or anachronistic interpretation. We have the duty to practically 'translate' the meaning of the texts for our modern times, because the Bible contains the Word of God, but in the words of human beings. Therefore, *a dialogue between the context of the biblical texts and that of the reader* would enable a meaningful reading of the Bible. A contextual reading of the Bible is a must if one wishes to understand the dialogue-friendly nature of the Bible.

Does the Bible Promote an Exclusivist Religion?

Quite a number of people are still taking it for granted that the Bible advocates a religion of exclusivism. The possible reasons for such a faulty position can be many: One possible reason could be that the Bible is 'super-cultural,'[9] that is to say that the biblical revelation is totally independent of every cultural influence and therefore it must be accepted as such without relating it to any cultural contexts. Consequently, also the religion promoted by the Bible is above all cultures and extra-contextual and therefore it is exclusively unique. However, we know that the Bible is neither super-cultural nor does it advocate any one form of culture. The biblical texts and their interpretations down the centuries have adapted and assimilated into the many cultures they have confronted.[10]

A second reason is drawn from the self-awareness of the people of Israel as chosen people which gave rise to negative judgments about other religions as vain idolatry. This involves one of the large theological themes of the Old Testament, namely, 'election theology'. It is true that the Old Testament speaks of the people of Israel as a 'specially chosen' people of God (Ex 19:3-8; Deut 7:6-7; Amos 3:1-2). However, from the context of 'election' of the people of Israel which begins with the call of Abraham it is made clear that the election and the promise attached to it is not limited to the people of Israel alone but is supposed to be extended to all peoples (cf. Gen 12:3: 'in thee shall all the tribes of the earth be blessed'). Thus, the fact of being the chosen people of God impels the people of Israel to be missionaries who would further reach out the blessings to 'all' the peoples of the earth. Thus, election implies not only a privilege but also a duty to relate to people of other cultures and religions.

The third reason is a sense of self-identity and authority of the New Testament people who inherit the similar kind of self-awareness like that of the people of Israel. They saw themselves as the new 'chosen race' and the 'new Israel' who have in the last times inherited the promises made by God to the people of Israel and who saw themselves as missionaries committed to converting everyone to the 'new way of life.' They did not consider it important to enter into any kind of 'dialogue' with any of the religions prevalent at that time. The NT texts like Jn 14:6 (I am the way, the truth and love), 1 Tim 2:5 (one mediator), Acts 4:12 (no other name - cf. 1 Jn 4:14; Jn 1:29), 1 Cor 8:5-6 (one God and one Lord - cf. Jn 3:16-17), Rev 22:13 (Jesus is the Alpha and Omega), Jn 1:2.14.18; Col 1:13-14.15.19-20; 2:9 (Jesus is the only Son of the Father), Col 1:24-27 (fullness of Christ's salvific mystery belongs also to the Church, inseparably united to her Lord which is his body - cf. 1 Cor 12:12-13.27; Col 1:18 - and thus Christ and the Church, though not identical, are inseparable - cf. 2 Cor 11:2; Eph 5:25-29; Rev 21:2.9 = Church as the bride of Christ), Mk 16:16; Jn 3:5; 1 Tim 2:3-4 (Church and Christ are necessary for salvation), Mk 16:15-16; Mt 28:18-20; Lk 24:46-48; Jn 17:18.20-21; Acts 1:8 (Christian Mission in universal) and Rom 1:5; 16:26 (Proper response is obedience of faith) are some of the difficult texts to understand and often misused by some people to promote exclusivist attitude in Christianity.

Encouraging 'Indicators' in the Old and in the New Testaments

The apparently exclusivist language used in the Bible is due to the efforts of the Lord to create a 'contrast' community, that is, a community that would follow values that are opposed to slavery and prostitution and practice concern for fellow humans and for the cosmos. As such three efforts of God to create such a contrast community can be identified in the Bible. The first was 'creation' itself; the second was 'the people of Israel as the covenantal community' and the third 'the Church as the new covenantal community.'[11] That is why the Bible (both the Old and New Testament), emphasizes the difference between the people of God (Israel and Christians) and the people of other cultures of the times. The call to be a contrast community does not make it an exclusivist one but one that would seek 'real' God and ultimate truth.

In fact, one can find any number of texts and stories in the Bible which contain and promote the spirit of dialogue with other religions. In the following we shall try to identify those elements in the Bible which we call as 'encouraging indicators of dialogue.' These indicators promote a spirit of dialogue on the one hand and on the other they would simultaneously clarify some of the objections raised against the 'dialogue-friendliness' of the Bible.

'Dialogical' God of the Bible

The God of the Bible is a 'dialogical God'. He dialogues with the human beings and with the cosmos. He is not merely a supreme, sovereign God who is high above the heavens but one who relates to the humans and tries to re-establish the order, harmony and equity. The whole of creation can be understood as God's negotiation with the 'disorder' found then. There are a number of dialogues between God and human beings in the story of the first parents and their descendants. The call of Abraham and the rest of the story of the Patriarchs are replete with dialogue between God and human beings. God continues this dialogue with the judges, prophets, kings and finally has spoken definitively in and through his Son Jesus Christ. And God will continue this dialogue with the human beings till the end of the world. If 'dialogue' is crucial for God, then the human beings who have been created in the 'image' of God should continue this dialogue not only with God but also with the fellow human beings.

The biblical story is not 'dictated' by God to the human beings which was then immediately written down. The history that the Bible tells is not critical but confessional history.[12] Such history tells us not about what actually took place in the history, but "what went on in what took place".[13] That is why the Bible is using a lot of 'foreign' literature to communicate the divinely revealed truths. Already in the primeval history the authors of the Bible are open enough to make use of the myths from their neighbouring Babylonian and Acadian literature.[14] Further, the experience of the people of God in Egypt and Babylon and the different encounters they made later under the Persians, Greeks and Romans have all strongly influenced the content and the language of the Bible considerably. Thus, considering the Bible as a literature which has taken about a thousand years before it got its final form, one can see that it is already a 'product' of a dialogue with the cultural milieu of the times.

Now we turn our attention to how the nations and outsiders are treated in the biblical story. Already from the promise made to Abraham where it is said that in him "*all the families of the earth* shall be blessed" (cf. Gen 12:3), it is made obvious that the nations are included as recipients of God's blessings. Commenting on this blessing to Abraham and to other Patriarchs, Rui de Menezes concludes that these blessings to the Patriarchs were also understood as "a blessing for all the clans and nations of the world."[15] In fact the promise made to Abraham concerning his descendants is not the only promise in the Book of Genesis. It also registers another promise made by God to Hagar concerning her son Ishmael.[16]

The call of Abraham and the promise made to him serves as the starting point and paves the way for the election of the people of Israel. As in the case of promise made to Abraham, so also the election of the people of Israel does not imply an exclusivist approach. It becomes clear when we consider the following two texts. In Deut 7:6-7 God gives the reason as to why he chose the people of Israel to be his treasured possession. It is not because they were one of the greatest people but because of his love for them though they were one of the fewest of all the people. "The high status bestowed on Israel is not just a merit but primarily a responsibility ... to serve as an example for other nations: Israel was chosen in order to bring light to the nations (Is 49:6-7; cf. 41:8-9; 42:2; 43:10; 44:1-2; 45:4)."[17] The second text is Amos 3:1-2 which also has the election of the people of Israel as its main theme, yet declares paradoxically[18] that they will be punished for all their iniquities. Both these texts forbid the people of Israel from becoming complacent and self-indulgent on the basis of their election. They should always remember that they were one of the most insignificant people and that they have to lead an accountable life.

In Ex 8:8.12.25.28; 9:28; 10:17-18, Yahweh listens to the request of Pharaoh made through Moses. In fact, Yahweh has 'come down' to liberate the Hebrews from Pharaoh who is actually oppressing them. *De facto* he has become the opponent to Yahweh who sends 'plagues' on Egyptians so that Pharaoh may be moved to allow the Hebrews to leave Egypt. When each of these plagues became unbearable for Pharaoh and the people of Egypt, Pharaoh requests Moses to pray to Yahweh to remove the plague with a promise that he would allow the Hebrews to leave Egypt. Though Pharaoh does not keep up his promise, still whenever Moses prayed to Yahweh on behalf of Pharaoh and Egyptians he listens to his prayer.

There are many other instances in the Old Testament which demonstrate its universal and inclusive direction. The 'great pilgrimage'[19] spoken of towards the end of the Book of Isaiah (cf. Is 66:18-21) at which an eschatological gathering of the nations will take place and the universal showering of the spirit of God on all humankind (cf. Joel 2:28-29) show the universal direction of God's mercy. Again the 'ten men' in Zech 8:23 who take hold of a Jew and confess that the God is with them represent 'all nations and tongues' and as in Is 66:18 here too the totality of non-Israelite world is implied by the phrase 'nations of every language'. Thus Zech 8:23 denotes an ever-broadening circle of people accounted for as part of Yahweh's redemptive scheme.[20] Here one could also call to mind the roles played by Balaam and Cyrus and his successor Darius in the history of salvation. Balaam prophesied in the name of Yahweh and 'blessed the people of Israel' though he was not an Israelite (cf. Num 22-24) and Cyrus and his successor Darius played a vital role in rebuilding the temple in Jerusalem.

One of the most significant instances of inclusiveness that we find in the Bible is the case of the so called *trias*, that is, the widow, the orphan and the stranger who are supposed to be taken care of by the Israelites (cf. Deut 24:17-21). Already Deut 10:18 presents the Lord himself as one who "executes justice for the orphan and the widow, and who loves the strangers, providing them food and clothing." Anna Norrbak in her meticulous research demonstrates that the duty to care for this *trias* of the Old Testament is not an additional duty but it is part of the covenantal obligation.[21]

Jealousy, Wrath and Vengeance of God?
Sometimes it claimed that the God of the Old Testament is a 'jealous' or 'zealous' God and therefore he cannot be a 'friendly' figure. However the 'jealous' or 'zealous' character attributed to him presents him as one who is concerned about restoring some 'affected' party (cf. Joel 2:18; Ezek 39:25) or as one who expresses his hostile feeling directed not only against the nations but also against the people of Israel themselves (cf. Ps 79:5-6; Ezek 38:19-23; Zeph 3:7-9; Zech 8:2-3; 1 Kg 14:22). In five texts this word is used attributively to Yahweh as 'jealous God' (cf. Ex 20:5; 34:14; Deut 4:24; 5:9; 6:15). All the five forbid the people of Israel from worshipping other gods and going after idol worship because such behaviour by the people of Israel reflected their infidelity to the covenant.

Both the Testaments of the Bible also speak of the wrath of God (cf. Ex 15:7; Deut 29:28; Jer 21:5; 32:37; Am 1:2-2:16; 4:6-11) which is again used to portray the God of the Bible as an 'unfriendly' person. In this regard we should make two important observations. Whenever the wrath of God is presented against the nations, that is, the non-Israelite people, then it is because the nations have protested against him. And whenever the people of Israel become the target of this wrath of God, it is aimed at chastising their unfaithful and stiff-necked behaviour so that they repent and return to the Lord. Further we read in Ex 32:9-14 that the Lord is capable of and does retain his wrath after intending to destroy the people as a response to their worship of the golden calf. The Lord was ready to spare the people of Sodom and Gomorrah if he would find at least ten righteous there (cf. Gen 18:32) and he changed his mind when he saw the Ninevites return from their wicked ways (cf. Jonah 3:10). The Book of Judges narrates a continuous story of God getting angry with his disobedient people and transforming his anger into mercy which impels him to send Judges to deliver the same people from the hands of their enemies (cf. Judg 2:11-12; 10:16).

When we move to the New Testament, the wrath of God is most fully explicated in the Epistle to the Romans in which it is said to be directed against human wickedness (Rom 1:18; 2:5-8).[22] As per the argumentative logic of the Epistle to the Romans, one would expect the revelation of the wrath of God from 3:21 that would take the form of a punishment, but what is actually revealed from Rom 3:21 is the righteousness of God through Jesus Christ. This righteousness means a 'new way' through which God himself takes the initiative and restores for humanity 'the right relationship' of it to himself.[23] It means that God is expressing his wrath in the form of an offer of salvation to human beings through the death and resurrection of Jesus Christ to everyone who is prepared to participate in the death and resurrection of Jesus Christ by faith. In other words, instead of wrath what is actually affected is a gratuitous grace of God which can be appropriated by every human being through faith.

Like jealousy and wrath, there is another characteristic of God reported about in both the Old and the New Testaments which appears to be hostile to the dialogue-friendliness of the Bible, namely, the 'vengeance of God'. It is not to be disputed that in the Bible, it is almost always God who is the subject who takes vengeance and at such moments he acts out of his royal authority. However, it should be noted that God does it to establish justice and to restore the affected party. In Lev 26:25; Is 1:24 and Is 59:17 God takes vengeance to establish justice among his people Israel, in Deut 32:35.41.43; Is 34:8; 47:3; 63:4; Jer 50-51, Ezek 25; in Mic 5:14 the purpose of divine vengeance is to liberate the people of God from the hands of their enemies; in Jer 5:9.29; 9:8; Ezek 24:8 it is used to deprive the enemies of their power and in Is 35:4 and Is 61:2 divine vengeance rescues those who have a fearful heart and comforts the mourning.

Rom 12:19 announces a ban on human beings taking revenge (cf. Deut 32:35; Lev 19:17-18; Heb 10:30) and demands that vengeance must be left to God, thereby qualifying vengeance as a recompense or repay. It explains fully the actual purpose of divine vengeance. Besides vengeance has to be left to God, because only he can recompense or repay proportionately. Further Lev 19:17-18 goes a step further and invites human beings to overcome evil with good. This whole concept of abstaining from vengeance and taking efforts to overcome evil with good is brought to its fulfilment by Jesus in Mt 5:43-48 where he calls for the love of enemies. Thus, we see that the anger and wrath of God against his people is only partial and temporal (cf. Is 54:7-8.10; Hos 11:5.8-9; and Mic 7:18-19) and they are all aimed at re-establishing justice, order and harmony.

Radically Universal Mission of Jesus

We should remember always that the Church was a post-resurrection reality and the New Testament contains post-resurrection faith-statements of the first Christian Community.

Though the New Testament presents post-resurrection, Christological views about Christ, still with the help of the New Testament Books we can arrive at a reasonably reliable picture of the historical Jesus who can be so to say sifted from the early Christian traditions. While sifting such traditions one should be careful not to draw arbitrary conclusions but take the text seriously and consider all possible sources. The so called principle of embarrassment[24] and the principle of multiple attestations[25] would be a good help in this regard. Here we consider such statements and incidents from the life of Jesus which provide us with a fair picture of the convictions and the proclamation of Jesus, though we are not going to scrutinize all the examples on the basis of the two above-mentioned principles. In any case all the examples we are considering in the following paragraphs reflect the 'radicality' of the universal mission of Jesus.[26]

First of all, we take the central proclamation of Jesus which is expressed in the Synoptic metaphor Kingdom of God or the Reign of God (cf. Mk 1:14-15). Though the hearers of Jesus were expecting a royal or a messianic ruler who would restore the rule over the people of Israel from the hands of the Romans, for Jesus the Reign of God meant not an outpouring of power but a revelation of the unconditional love of God. The proper response demanded by this proclamation is 'accepting God's unconditional love' which in turn calls for loving one's brothers and sisters unconditionally. Thus, Jesus' proclamation of the Kingdom of God does not aim at achieving political autonomy, but at practicing love which contains the true power and force of liberation. Theologically it implies that God is love (cf. 1 Jn 4:7-16) and philosophically love becomes the absolute value. Those who accept this proclamation of love become brothers and sisters by making the love of God present in their life. This is succinctly expressed by Gal 3:28 where Paul asserts that when someone is in Christ Jesus, then there is no distinction whatsoever between them, neither on the basis of religion nor race nor sex. This universal brotherhood can be extended to abolish the distinctions based on caste, colour, class and status. Even atheists can be considered to follow Jesus if only they would practice this love (*agapē*). However, making God's love present can take a variety of forms. The love (*agapē*) proclaimed by Jesus as the soul of God's Reign is an active and effective love. It means "doing good" to people by responding effectively to their needs,[27] that is, this love must be shown in action and not in empty words (cf. 1 Jn 3:17-18) and such actions should be beneficial to the recipients.

This proclamation of Jesus that God loves everyone without any condition and he is a 'loving' ruler is based on the 'Abba' experience of Jesus (cf. Mk 1:9-11; 14:36; Mt 11:25-27; cf. Rom 8:15; Gal 4:15).[28] As a consequence of this experience of God as Abba Jesus gains insurmountable freedom to love all human beings as brothers and sisters, (Mt 23:8-10; cf. Gal 3:28) and is able to rise above the challenge of the scribes and Pharisees on theological issues (Mk 2:1-3.6; 12:13-40) but at the same time respecting them as persons and relating to them in a friendly manner by accepting their invitations to share a meal with them (Lk 7:36; Mk 12:28-34; Lk 13:31). He breaks the traditional ritual and purity boundaries and celebrates table-fellowship with tax-collectors and sinners without any aversion towards sinners (Lk 15:1-2; Mt 21:31) and demonstrates a special concern for little ones (Mk 9:42).

He calls ordinary people to be his close friends and among the twelve disciples who were very intimately related to him one can identify a variety of background. One of them was a Zealot (Lk 6:15), another a tax-collector (Mt 9:9), a few were disciples of John the Baptist (Jn 1:29-51) and a few more were fishermen. Though opposed to riches (Mk 10:23-27; Lk 13:17-21; Mt 6:24), Jesus is friendly to Zacchaeus, Joseph of Arimathea and to Nicodemus. He was so free that he questioned the established structural authority both religious (cf. Mt 23) and political (Lk 13:32). Contrary to the custom of the time his attitude to women was very positive, he had women disciples who accompanied him during his ministry (Lk 8:1-2), and during his passion, death and resurrection (cf. Mk 15:40.47; 16:1-8), he shows kindness to the widow of Nain (cf. Lk 7:11.17), he makes it a point to praise as exemplary the faith of the woman who was healed from her haemorrhage (cf. Mk 5:25-34) and he did not hesitate to request a Samaritan woman for a drink (cf. Jn 4). Jesus' dialogue with the Samaritan woman also indicates a universalization of the reign of God to all peoples (Jn 4:1-6). Here too Jesus is amazed at the openness of the woman to tell the truth and her thirst for 'living water' (Jn 4:7-15).

He appreciates Samaritans (Lk 9:51-56; 17:11-19; Jn 4) though the relationship between Jews and the Samaritans was one of mutual hatred at that time. The story of the Good Samaritan (Lk 10:29-37) and the healing of the ten lepers (Lk 17:11-14) present the Samaritans in the more privileged position than the Jews who are also part of these narratives. The faith of the centurion of Capernaum (Mt 8:5-13) is praised as greater than anyone else in Israel. And the entry of the 'others' in the banquet (Mt 22:1-14; Lk 14:15-24) symbolising the universal pilgrimage of the Book of Isaiah (Is 66) demonstrates that with faith and conversion one gets access into the reign of God (Mk 1:15). However, what is being appreciated in all these passages is not a movement towards and adherence to a particular religion but a conversion to the God of life, love and freedom. Another instance when Jesus marvels at the faith of the pagans is the case of the Canaanite woman (Mt 15:21-28). Though Jesus appears initially to be insulting the woman from a 'racist' prejudice, still he learns his lesson on the enlarged vision of God from this pagan woman. In which case what Jesus has said concerning the food and the dogs (cf. Mk 7:27) can be understood as a 'provocative challenge.' Finally, Jesus rewards her humble but great response by casting out the demon from her daughter (cf. Mk 7:28-29).

There is yet another story of a non-disciple casting out demons in the name of Jesus (Mk 9:38-39) which serves as evidence of the borderless universality of the Reign of God. Though the disciples try the strategy of exclusivism, Jesus corrects them and widens their perspective by advising them not to prevent this non-disciple from doing good. Thus, through the words and deeds of Jesus we learn that those whom the centre of power held by the religious authorities considered to be beyond salvation have come to occupy the central place in the reign of God.[29]

In fact, Jesus attempted a renewal of his religion by relativizing all the established structures and wanted to promote an adoration of God "in spirit and truth" (Jn 4:23). All that he said and did centred on the metaphor of reign of God. It implied a total reorientation of all relationships, both with God and fellow human beings, in accordance with God's intention. As we have seen a number of gospel episodes make it clear that Jesus wished a universalization of the reign of God.

Universal Mission Continued?

After Jesus the disciples who formed a movement around him became a community that was called as *ekklesia* (Mt 16:18; 18:18) and it took it upon itself to proclaim the 'good news' brought about by him. However, while Jesus proclaimed the reign of God as his central message, the early community of disciples started proclaiming Jesus himself as the central kerygma. By and by this community was getting the shape of a structured institution with its hierarchical structures and began to struggle to keep up with the radical ways of Jesus. In fact, this community or the Church was supposed to proclaim the reign of God, as Paul does under house arrest in Rome (cf. Acts 28:30-31). To a large extent the Church succeeded in remaining faithful to the proclamation of Jesus and spreading the love preached and lived by Jesus. Evidences of such proclamation can be found in the Sermon on the Mount which sounds like "the charter of the Reign of God in its universality and openness to whoever is willing to enter it"[30] and in passages like Gal 5:13-14 and Rom 13:8-10 which insist on the love of neighbour as an essential consequence of one's belongingness to Jesus Christ. Yet as a distinct religious group the Church started perceiving Jews as dishonest group (Mt 27:24-25) and paganism as culpable idolatry (Rom 1:18-32). The Pharisees were seen and opposed as outright enemies of the Church (Mt 23:3-36) and in writings like the Household Codes (Eph 5:21-6:9; Col 3:18-4:1; 1 Tim 2:1-7.8-15; 5:1-2; 6:1-2; 4; Tit 2:4-5; 1 Pet 2:13-3:12; Col 3:18-4:1) the sexist biases were not totally removed.[31] And the radical inter-human concern proclaimed by Jesus is altered and a preferential love for Christians is advocated (cf. 1 Thess 5:15; Gal 6:10: 'let us work for the good of all, and especially for those of the family of faith').

Such instances depict the Church's inability to live up to the radical freedom of Jesus and to Church's 'little faith' (Mt 8:26; 14:31; 16:8)[32] and which is understandable of a pilgrim Church in its fledgling stage. Such a toning down the radicality of Jesus could be due to the persecution the early Church experienced or to the charismatic phenomena it experienced or to the apocalyptic world-view it shared.[33] Yet there are a number of instances recorded in the New Testament which present that the early Church had not totally lost the universal direction of the mission of Jesus.

The whole incident at the house of Cornelius demonstrates that God shows no partiality (Acts 10:34-35; cf. Rom 2:11; Deut 10:17) and Peter crosses over into a territory of God where all people are considered pure, including Cornelius. In this story the Gentiles became the occasion for Peter to cross over to the territory of God by whom all are created and saved in Jesus Christ. Secondly the whole controversy over 'circumcision' as a precondition for baptism that was a serious concern of the Christians in Antioch in Syria was solved in an amicable way with mutual respect and by including all parties concerned (cf. Acts 15). In Rom 1:18-2:29 though Paul is actually finding fault with the Gentiles that they have failed to recognize and praise God through creation and through the law engraved in their hearts (Rom 2:14-16; cf. Jer 31:31-34), thereby he indirectly admits that the revelation of God includes all human beings. Elsewhere in the same epistle Paul also speaks that real circumcision is of the heart (Rom 2:26-29). Paul's speech in Lystra (Acts 14:16-17) and in Athens (Acts 17:22-31) accept a pre-Christian revelation of God through other channels. Such a search for God is a gift of God.

The Acts of the Apostles and the epistles of Paul especially the epistle to Galatians make a clear distinction between the Jewish and the Gentile mission of the early Church. The mission to the Jews of the first Palestinian followers of Jesus was radically different from the centrifugal Gentile mission initiated by the Jewish Hellenistic Christian communities of the Diaspora, and Paul's understanding of mission was very different from that of John.[34] The difference in the different kinds of missionary strategies followed by the missionaries in the early Church serves must be attributed to the difference in the nature of the target groups. For example, the way the 'conversion of Paul' is presented in Acts 22:6-11 and in Acts 26:1-18. The former has a 'Jewish' character because its addressees are the Jews in Jerusalem and the latter embodies a 'universal' because the addressee there is King Agrippa.

1 Tim 2:4: *God desires everyone to be saved and to come to the knowledge of the truth*

We would like to look at this text which speaks of God's universal plan of salvation which appears to include everyone in the economy of salvation. This instruction occurs in the context of instructions on prayer. Along with Rom 3:27-31 and 11:26-32 this verse is considered to be the 'most inclusive and universal of Paul's statements' concerning the will of God for human salvation.[35] V 4 has God's universal intention, as opposed to some form of exclusivism that is mainly in mind. The first verb in v 4, namely 'desire' refers to a strong will of God. Second, the purpose of the reference to "all people" is made with the Pauline mission to the gentiles in mind and is against any kind of exclusivist Torah-centred approach and a downplaying of the Gentile mission. Thirdly, though the theological and eschatological elements of salvation persist in this text, yet the primary concern in Ephesus is focused on building a people of God who incorporate all people regardless of ethnic, social, or economic backgrounds, and who are characterised by a manner of life that is qualitatively different from that of society at large.[36] Finally, the phrase 'knowledge of truth' refers to the 'true understanding of the Gospel' which is actually at stake in Ephesus. Here Paul is drawing a contrast between his Gospel and that of his rivals.[37] Further, this phrase expresses the cognitive process of knowing and the idea of conversion as a rational decision to embrace the truth. Here truth refers to God's authoritative revelation. Thus 'coming' to the knowledge of the truth combines a statement about the quality of the gospel message and commitment to it.

In fact the universal perspective of the text begins already in 2:1 where Paul instructs his readers to pray on behalf of everyone including kings and all in high position[38] which is then justified theologically in v 3 asserting that such a prayer for everyone is 'right' and 'acceptable' in the sight of God. Such prayers for all people contains a more expansive universal vision than the one expressed in texts like 1 Thess 4:9 and Gal 6:10 (see above) which advocate a preferential love for the members of the community. And this universal direction of the text is finally corroborated by making two assertions in v 5: namely that God is one and that Jesus is the one mediator by the fact of being human. That God is one is an indispensable foundation for uniting human beings as children of one and the same father. The second assertion that Jesus the mediator is himself a human being is even more interesting, because instead of referring to the distinguishing aspects of Jesus' mediator-ship, Paul here speaks of Jesus as a human being which could be a converging point for all human beings. This is something similar to the way he has presented the grace received through one man in Rom 5:12-21.

Bible Promotes Ecumenism

The ecumenical movement's effort[39] to restore the unity of God's people is profoundly based on Scripture. Such an objective was the constant concern of the Lord (Jn 10:16 speaks of "one flock and one shepherd"; 17:11 of Christ's prayer "that they may be one"; 17:22 of the continued prayer of Christ "that they may be one, as we are one"). Further union of Christians in faith, hope and love (Eph 4:2-5), in mutual respect (Phil 2.1-5) and solidarity (1 Cor 12:14-27: 'the solidarity of the Christians that through many, yet one body'; cf. Rom 12:4-5) which is founded in an organic union in Christ after the manner of vine and branches (Jn 15:4-5), Head and members (Eph 1:22-23; 4:12-16) is a biblical requirement. Such a union must be perfect in the likeness of that between the Father and the Son. The theological foundation for such union is provided by,

> Eph 4:4-6: *"There is one body and one Spirit, just as you were called to the one hope of your calling, one Lord, one faith, one baptism, one God and Father of all, who is above all and through all and in all. But each of us was given grace according to the measure of Christ's gift."*

> and Gal 3:27-28: *"As many of you as were baptized into Christ have clothed yourselves with Christ. There is no longer Jew or Greek, there is no longer slave or free, there is no longer male and female; for all of you are one in Christ Jesus").*

Pope Francis in his address at the conclusion of the synod of Bishops on the family on Saturday, 24th October 2015 said that the Synod was "about bearing witness to everyone that, for the Church, the Gospel continues to be a vital source of eternal newness, against all those who would "indoctrinate" it in dead stones to be hurled at others."[40] Taking inspiration from this statement of the Pope, when we read the Holy Bible with an open mind, we realize that there are a number of elements and aspects which motivate and encourage to enter into an active dialogue with people of all religions. Such a dialogue implies no intentions of 'subduing' other religions nor 'surrendering' oneself to them. The Bible demands that all those who hold it as their Sacred Scriptures must be prepared to dialogue with others with an open mind and share the God-Experience that is mediated by it.

Whether one likes it or not, to be religious in the Indian context is to be interreligious. One cannot live here as though the others do not exist. Let us take the biblical story seriously which demands that we follow the example of a dialogical God, merciful God, listening to the others with authentic concern, seeking justice, following a spirituality of involvement, forgiving even the enemies, remaining open for change, including strangers and foreigners, helping the needy, rooted in the Father (Theocentric - Ultimate Reality), ready to take risk and carry the cross, seeking solidarity with the underprivileged, remaining non-judgemental, self-critical, non-legalistic, reconciliatory and loving (agape = selfless love = active and effective concern).

Endnotes

[1] The etymological root of this word 'religion' is either *religare* (Latin) which means 'to bind' implying a communion between members of the same religion or *relegere* (Latin) which means 'to go through or over again in reading, speech or thought' or 'read again, reread' in the sense of making an inquiry which implies a 'conscientious scruple.' For s detailed analysis of these two terms cf. Sarah F. Hoyt, "The Etymology of Religion," in *Journal of the American Oriental Society* 32,2 (1912): 126-9. In our text here 'religion' is understood in the phenomenological sense as 'an outward form as to how human beings relate to God' which is expressed through rites and ceremonies such as 'prayer' 'cult' and 'sacrifice.' Here 'God' and 'divine realities' are considered to be the objects of religion. Cf. H.

Fries, "Religion," in *Lexikon Für Theologie Und Kirche VIII* (Freiburg: Herder, 1986), 1164.

[2] Sometimes tolerance in the religious sphere is considered to be a valid 'recognition of the doctrines of others even when they are contradictory to one's own convictions.' Cf. Joseph Veliyathil, "Religious Tolerance in India," *The Living Word* 78,5 (September-October 1972):352.

[3] Jay Newman, The Idea of Religious Tolerance, American Philosophical Quarterly 15 (3), University of Illinois Press, 1978, 188-89. In this well spelt out article the author has successfully clarified the meaning of religious tolerance.

[4] Congregation For the Doctrine of Faith, *Declaration "Dominus Jesus" on the Unity and Salvific Universality of Jesus Christ and the Church 2*, accessed on 08.04.2017 from http://www.vatican.va/roman_curia/congregations/cfaith/documents/rc_con_cfaith_doc_20000806_dominus-iesus_en.html

[5] *An Attitude of the Church Towards the Followers of Other Religions*, Secretariat for Non-Christian Religions, Vatican City, 1984, n. 4.

[6] However, it must also be admitted that of late such a harmonious living is suffering a setback due to religious fundamentalism and politicisation of religions not necessarily from the Christian mainline Churches.

[7] Soares-Prabhu G. M., "Religion and Communalism: The Christian Dilemma," in: *Biblical Themes For A Contextual Theology Today*, Collected Writings of George M. Soares-Prabhu S.J., Vol I, Isaac Padinjarekuttu (ed.), 1999, 173-190.

[8] D. Senior and C. Stuhlmueller, *The Biblical Foundations for Mission* (Maryknoll, N.Y.: Orbis Books, 1983), 344-47.

[9] Cf. Joseph Ratzinger, *Truth and Tolerance: Christian Belief and World Religions, trans.* Henry Taylor (San Francisco: Ignatius Press, 2004), 122.

[10] For a more detailed understanding on the mutual influence of culture and Bible, see Lucien Legrand, "Inculturation in the Bible," in Mario Saturnino Dias (ed.), *Rooting Faith in Asia. Source Book for Evangelization*, Quezon City: Claretian Publications, 2005, 209-222.

[11] Cf. Soares-Prabhu G. M., "Expanding the Horizon of Christian Mission: A Biblical Perspective," in: *Biblical Themes For A Contextual Theology Today*, Collected Writings of George M. Soares-Prabhu S.J., Vol I, Isaac Padinjarekuttu (ed.), 1999, 3-15.

[12] Cf. Gerhard Von Rad, *Old Testament Theology*, vol. 1 (Edinburg: Oliver and Boyd, 1962), 108.

[13] John Marsh, *The Gospel of John* (Harmondsworth: Penguin, 1968), 18.

[14] Cf. Soare-Prabhu G. M., *Expanding the Horizon*, 4.

[15] Rui de Menezes, *The Global Vision of the Hebrew Bible* (Bombay: St. Pauls, 2010), 54.

[16] See Gen 16:10: "[10] The angel of the LORD also said to her, "I will so greatly multiply your offspring that they cannot be counted for multitude."

[17] Moshe Weinfeld, *Deuteronomy 1-11: A New Translation with Introduction and Commentary*, The Anchor Bible (New York: Doubleday, 1991), 367.

[18] There is an apparent paradox in this verse because on the one hand it speaks about the election of the people of Israel which is actually supposed to bring them blessing but here what the verse is promising is not any blessing but punishment for the iniquities. Cf. Francis I. Anderson, David Noel Freedman, *Amos: A New Translation with Introduction and Commentary*, The Anchor Bible (New York: Doubleday, 1989), 32.

[19] John D. W. Watts, *Isaiah 34-66*, Word Biblical Commentary 25 (Texas: Word Books, 1987), 357-358.

[20] Cf. Carol L. Meyers, Eric M Meyers, *Haggai, Zechariah 1-8: A New Translation with Introduction and Commentary*, The Anchor Bible (New York: Doubleday, 1987), 441.

[21] Cf. Anna Norrbak, *The Fatherless and the Widow in the Deuteronomic Covenant* (Abo Akademi University Press, 2001).

[22] Cf. G. L. Borchert, "Wrath, Destruction," *Dictionary of Paul and His Letters* eds. Gerals F. Hawthorne, Ralph P. Martin and Daniel G. Reid (Illinois: IVP, 1993), 991.

[23] Cf. Joseph A. Fitzmyer, *Romans: A New Translation with Introduction and Commentary*, The Anchor Bible (New York: Doubleday, 1993), 341.

[24] This principle means that the books of the New Testament contain statements und expressions which clearly 'contradict' the traditions of the time, and thus would have been embarrassing for the first hearers and readers of the same. Since such statements have been included in the New Testament in spite of the fact that they contradict the existing traditions, these must have their origin in Jesus Christ.

[25] The principle of multiple attestations means that a statement or an incident in the New Testament is attested to by more than one text and therefore it must really have happened in the life of Jesus or in case of the assertions they must have been truly spoken by Jesus himself.

[26] Cf. G. M. Soares-Prabhu, "The Unprejudiced Jesus and the Prejudiced Church," in: *Biblical Spirituality of Liberative Action*, Collected Writings of George M. Soares-Prabhu S.J., Vol III, Scaria Kuthirakkattel (ed.), 2003, 163-172.

[27] Cf. G. M. Soares-Prabhu, "The Synoptic Love-Commandment: The Dimensions of Love in the Teaching of Jesus," *Jeevadhara* 13/74 (1983), 85-103.

[28] Cf. G. M. Soares-Prabhu, "The Dharma of Jesus," in: *Biblical Spirituality of Liberative Action*, Collected Writings of George M. Soares-Prabhu S.J., Vol III, Scaria Kuthirakkattel (ed.), 2003, 3-4.

[29] C. S. Song, *Jesus in the Power of the Spirit* (Minneapolis: Fortress Press, 1994), 77-78.

[30] Jacques Dupuis, *Christianity and the Religions: From Confrontation to Dialogue*, (Maryknoll: Orbis Books, 2002), 29.

[31] However, it must be noted here that while the Moral philosophers like Aristotle used the so called household codes to advise their male readers on how to govern and subordinate their wives, children and slaves, the similar codes in the New Testament depart significantly from their previous model by addressing also wives and children as subjects and obliging the *Pater Familias* to certain amount of mutual commitment in the relationships. Cf. Keener in C. S. Keener, "Man and Woman," *DPL* (Leicester: Inter Varsity Press, 1993), 587.

[32] Cf. G. M. Soares-Prabhu, "The Unprejudiced Jesus and the Prejudiced Church," 168.

[33] Ibid, 168-169.

[34] Cf. Lucien Legrand, *Unity and Plurality: Mission in the Bible* (Pune: Ishvani Publications, 1992), 101-137.

[35] Cf. Luke Timothy Johnson, *The First and Second Letters to Timothy: A New Translation with Introduction and Commentary,* The Anchor Bible (New York: Doubleday, 2001), 191.

[36] Cf. Philip H. Towner, *The Letters to Timothy and Titus* (Grand Rapids, Michigan: William B. Eerdmans, 2006), 177.

[37] Cf. Luke Timothy Johnson, *The First and Second Letters to Timothy*, 191.

[38] The inclusion of kings and rulers in the Christian prayer combines the refusal to acknowledge earthly princes as divine and the duties of good

citizenship. Cf. Luke Timothy Johnson, *The First and Second Letters to Timothy*, 194.

[39] Cf. Joseph A Fitzmyer, The Biblical Commission's Document "The Interpretation of the Bible in the Church": Text and Commentary, Roma 1995, 186-188.

[40] From the Address of His Holiness Pope Francis on the occasion of the Conclusion of the Family Synod, accessed on 15.08.2016, from: http://w2.vatican.va/content/francesco/en/speeches/2015/october/documents/papa-francesco_20151024_sinodo-conclusione-lavori.html.

Mercy: A Key-category for the Spirituality of Dialogue

Ambrogio Bongiovanni

Spirituality of Dialogue and Dialogue of Spirituality

After fifty years from the promulgation of *Nostra Aetate* ("In Our Time"), the Declaration of the Second Vatican Council on the relation between the Church and non-Christian religions (28 October 1965), the concept of inter-religious dialogue seems to be eagerly entered not only into the language of the Church and of other religious traditions, but also into society and politics.

Though not all Christians, whether clergy or laity are indeed convinced of its importance, dialogue is seen as the main instrument to build a new human society. Rather, it would represent the most positive aspect in the era of globalization and of the increased proximity of peoples, in the complex, problematic and uncertain scenario of our times.

Nevertheless, it is not at all taken for granted that interreligious dialogue be automatically practised. Notwithstanding its political or diplomatic manipulation, interreligious dialogue has to be understood as a "religious dialogue", founded on God, developed within and between the religious experiences, in the search of truth and through the spirituality of the encounter with the "other".

What renders dialogue authentically 'religious' is spirituality, with its power to draw out and to face a diversity of experiences. Spirituality is indeed the driving force that encourages the participants of our encounters and seminars that have been conducting in India and Italy for the last twenty years, by means of a partnership of organizations, especially the support and encouragement of Movimento S. Francesco Saverio, and individuals: scholars, teachers, students and social activists.

John Paul II pointed out clearly that "the spirituality [...] involves the concept of man's quest for a personal relationship with God, a relationship which can give life and substance to his relations with others who follow a different religious tradition."[1]

Nostra Aetate developed the thought on the need of a new relationship from the basic human quest, common to all humankind, at the foundation of the search for truth:

> "Men look to their different religions for an answer to the unsolved riddles of human existence... What is man? What is the meaning and purpose of life? What is upright behaviour, and what is sinful? Where does suffering originate, and what end does it serve? How can genuine happiness be found? What happens at death? What is judgment? What reward follows death? And finally, what is the ultimate mystery, beyond human explanation, which embraces our entire existence, from which we take our origin and towards which we tend?"[2]

To some documents of the Catholic Church dialogue is lived in four forms in which it can develop: dialogue of life, dialogue of co-operation, formal dialogue or exchanges among experts, and dialogue of spirituality. Though all the four forms are important, "dialogue of spirituality can contribute a depth and quality which will preserve these from the danger of mere activism."[3]

But I think that the most essential aspect to be pointed out here is that dialogue is a living dialogue. Shifting from the doctrinal to the spiritual dimension implies the shift from a prevailing idea that religious systems are able to dialogue towards a 'relational' approach: dialogue is possible only when there are 'persons'[4] ready and available to be involved in it and to share their living faith. In this sense it seems to me more appropriate to stress the term 'inter-faith' instead of 'inter-religious'. It is not just a matter of terms: inter-faith-dialogue and inter-religious-dialogue are part of the same coin, but they are not the same face of the coin! In fact, we can say that dialogue belongs to two distinct levels. Firstly, a 'dialogue-activity', based on elements of 'rationality', conscious of the distinct goals to be attained, oriented to a common platform of values (*ethos*) for concrete steps of communities and societies. Secondly, a 'dialogue-relationship', which is based on people for whom the spirit of dialogue is a 'rule of life'. In the first form, inter-personal communication amongst participants remains only on the background, while in the second form, the partners in dialogue are involved with their lives in a decisive manner. The two levels complement each other, even if the emphasis is often unbalanced on the 'dialogue-activity'. We must insist however that, without the 'dialogue-relationship', the 'dialogue-activity' would be hollow, devoid of content, ideals, momentum and spirituality.[5] In fact, spirituality "is more than knowledge and discussion. It is inseparable from the search for holiness which, in the absolute sense, belongs only to God, but which, through his tender mercy, is given also to man as a gift and a responsibility. The Second Vatican Council has re-echoed the exhortation of St. Paul: 'What God wants is for you all to be holy' (1 Thess. 4,3), underlining on more than one occasion the universal vocation to holiness (cf. *Lumen Gentium*, 42)".

> "Thus, the theme of spirituality constitutes a natural meeting point for the followers of different religious traditions and a fruitful subject for interreligious dialogue. [...] "dialogue of spirituality" is an essential and crowning form of dialogue between men and women of different religious experiences. It enables "persons rooted in their own religious traditions" to share "their spiritual riches, for instance with regard to prayer and contemplation, faith and ways of searching for God or the Absolute"".[6]

At the same time, we have to distinguish the spirituality of dialogue from the dialogue of spirituality. Indeed, different spiritualities may deeply meet and be nourishing thanks to the spirituality of dialogue, namely "a vision capable of sustaining the efforts to promote good and harmonious relations between the followers of different religions. Interreligious dialogue is never easy. It requires solid convictions and a great understanding and sensitivity regarding difference."[7]

Mercy: a key-category for dialogue

In our previous seminar in Hyderabad (2014)[8] I dealt with some aspects of the *dialogic principle*, a fundamental principle for interfaith spirituality, which is theologically founded on God himself, from a Christian perspective, on the Trinity and on the self-revelation of God to his creatures. The comprehension of this principle brings about two concrete implications for all Christians: *openness* (to otherness and truth) and the *kenosis (self-emptiness or self-renunciation)*.

Following on from the transcendent origin of dialogue, the Jubilee Year of Mercy, called by Pope Francis, has made me ask: what is the relationship between *mercy*, an essential attribute of God, especially in the three Abrahamic religions, and dialogue? Is it appropriate to consider *mercy* as a key-category for the spirituality of interfaith dialogue?[9]

I think that we can respond positively to both questions, considering dialogue in its deepest meaning, namely in its spiritual and existential dimension. Revisiting the meaning of mercy will help us to understand the spirit of dialogue in various situations of life.

The Jewish origin of the word mercy is *rahamim* indicating the "innards" and in particular, in its conjugation in the singular, is referred to the "womb". So, it metaphorically indicates the deep relationship, I would say 'intense' relationship, between the mother and the child or between people with a strong bond, like a family bond, or the deep love of any long-lasting relationship, beyond any calculation and reason of interests and duties. If we think this relationship as referred to God, it means much more. Even if human frailty provoked the negligence of a mother for her child, God never would forget each and all of his creatures.

> "Can a mother forget her infant, be without tenderness for the child of her womb? Even should she forget, I will never forget you". (Isaiah 49,15)

If we juxtapose *hesed* at the word *rahamim*, then mercy indicates an ontological dimension of God: namely his goodness, his love:

> "I will espouse you to me forever: I will espouse you in right and in justice, in love and in mercy [*hesed*]; I will espouse you in fidelity, and you shall know the Lord". (Hosea 2,18-19)

The reference to mercy is for Christians the awareness of the infinite love of God at the basis of Creation itself. Mercy goes beyond the 'carnality' of human generation. Moreover, we can also say that the topological indication of *rahamim* refers to the place where life is received and carefully kept: reception or welcome as a starting point for strong relationships.

In the Bible mercy is the highest attribute of God, as recalled in the New Testament (Ef.2,4), "God is rich in mercy", explaining his universal plan of salvation. Christianity simply summarizes this in the expression: "God is love".

> "For as the heavens tower over the earth, so his mercy towers over those who fear him. As far as the east is from the west, so far has he removed our sins from us. As a father has compassion on his children, so the LORD has compassion on those who fear him"". (Psalm 103, 11-13).

And, on top of that, God addressed his love to any human being until he himself took the weak human condition (*kenosis* of God) in Jesus Christ.

Forgetting or unaware of this, we human beings often build an anthropocentric god, with our measure, neglecting the central theme of creation in Genesis (which is also found in the *Qur'ān*), of a human in the image of God: the nature of human being is in God himself which gives the full dignity to become a human person, capable of relating to others and to God.

John Paul II, at the very beginning of his pontificate, dedicated his encyclical *Dives in Misericordia* (1980) to the theme of mercy. At the n. 7 of the encyclical we read:

> "Believing in the crucified Son means "seeing the Father," means believing that love is present in the world and that this love is more powerful than any kind of evil in which individuals, humanity, or the world are involved. Believing in this love means believing in mercy. For mercy is an indispensable dimension of love; it is as it were love's second name and, at the same time, the specific manner in which love is revealed and effected *vis-a-vis* the reality of the evil that is in the world, affecting and besieging man, insinuating itself even into his heart and capable of causing him to "perish in Gehenna""

So, mercy represents also a revelatory event.[10]

In Islam the mercy of God is among the most mentioned attributes. To remind believers the nature of God and his concern for humanity, every *sura* of the *Qur'ān*, except the ninth, begins with the expression *"bismi'llah al- Rahman al- Rahim"*, "in the name of God (*Allah*), Clement and Merciful". The Qur'ān says that God's mercy is bestowed on each individual. It is significant the following sura:

> "And He it is Who sendeth the winds as tidings heralding His mercy, till, when they bear a cloud heavy (with rain), We lead it to a dead land, and then cause water to descend thereon and thereby bring forth fruits of every kind. Thus, bring We forth the dead. Haply ye may remember" (Qur'ān 7,57).[11]

Also, in other Asian religious traditions we find significant aspects of mercy, which must be understood, contextualized and valued, offering a contribution to the spirituality of dialogue and to Christians the chance to learn from other spiritualities and to broaden the horizons of understanding God's mercy.

In Hinduism, for instance, the doctrine of the Love of God is proposed by the *Ṛgveda* (IX, 32.5) and the veneration to God as life sustainer is expressed in *Ṛgveda* (V, 1.1). Particularly the book *Bhagavad-gītā* and its central message, the *bhakti* as the supreme love of God which means a consecration of the life of the believer and all his activities to him, exerted a beneficial influence on the entire Hindu religious system. *Bhakti*, which represents the most popular spirituality and mystics of Hinduism, is founded on the intimate spiritual experience of the greatness, the bounty (mercy) and grace of God (*prasāda*). It is only through *prasāda* that *bhakti* becomes effective and salvific. The grace works in the intimacy of man, provoking in him the dispositions favourable to the divine union, removing everything that hinders or delays his spiritual progress and finally gives him the supreme *bhakti* that culminates in his final liberation.[12]

In this search, mercy might be seen as a 'common' category or an epistemological ground for the spirituality of dialogue. It is not enough to proclaim the mercy of God which seems to be a unifying factor for Christians and believers of other religious traditions. In fact, we have also to interpret and understand the differences and meanings even in terms of practical implications and living faith. That is the dialogue of spiritualities. First of all, this falls in the responsibility of the believers of each religious tradition to testify to others their views (dialogue). As a Christian, commenting, for example, on the parable of the prodigal son (Gospel of Luke 15.11-32), the way the father shows his love for both his children is a sign of the mercy God for everyone. But the parable also makes clear the movement of love of the father, a concrete action taken. It is the father who takes the initiative and welcomes his "lost" son. This teaches us that we have not to wait for the Day of Judgment to come for the mercy and forgiveness of God. The lost son realized that he was forgiven only because his father went to meet him (*mercy*), who took the first step, showing him that he wanted to leave the past behind (*reconciliation*).

The teaching of the Gospel shows once more that the fundamental *openness* of God, as discussed earlier, towards human beings, towards the other, and even towards the misery and weakness of the human condition. That openness comes from love and reaches its climax precisely on the Cross.

However, mercy finds a lot of obstacles in all contexts. Unfortunately, as Cardinal Poupard remembered, for most of the ancient philosophers (Plato, Aristotle, Seneca) mercy was not just a virtue, rather it was seen as weakness and dialogue was only linked to the world of ideas. That 'ancient' way of thinking is still alive today in Western European societies, which, although often appealing officially to the Judeo-Christian values, they do not effectively propose that fabric of values or even do not look outside of their own cultural contexts. Indeed, Europe seems often imprisoned by the obsessions of the past, especially with respect to Islam, incapable to reconcile the present with the past. In a similar way, other peoples outside Europe show that obsession towards Europe, perhaps for other reasons, or within their own contexts in reference to other communities or situations. In my opinion, the clashes taking place today almost in every corner of our world, are not between different civilizations (as some have claimed to call) but they are between 'obsessions' of one group against the other group, of a worldview against another worldview, of one community against another community. Before a threat or an attack, we respond with the old logic of revenge "eye for an eye", or of closed attitude. Unfortunately, war, terror and violence are the antithesis of mercy and dialogue and are unfortunately becoming today the only justified and 'rational' solution to resolve conflicts. But this approach shows a narrow and critical use of 'reason''. Where is 'reason' in this solution? That sadly shows a lack of human mercy and a betrayal of the mercy of God to which most of religions claim to refer to.

Mercy represents a real prophetic change. It is at the center of the conversion to God in response to the signs of the times and to the changes in every area of the world, in every time and place. Every time needs God's mercy to achieve reconciliation: conversion to look at and to be open to otherness with new eyes and hearts, with confidence, welcoming the other as a mother welcomes the life in her womb or as the father meets his "lost" son. That's a call to believers of all religious traditions to rediscover the meaning for themselves. That means also to rediscover the roots of the Christian faith.

In this way we can justify mercy as a *key-category* of dialogue. The spirituality of dialogue is characterized by the elements of God's mercy. Mercy produces dialogue and is the model for dialogue and helps us to live courageously even in the midst of conflicts or worries. In this sense, interfaith dialogue is a gift of God and becomes the historical praxis of God's mercy "in our time"!

In this way, dialogue becomes the space of reception, welcome, opening, of a profound encounter with the religiously 'other' in the search, in charity, of the truth of God, the beginning and ultimate end of humanity: truth which is receptive and lets the people meet and reveal; truth which is sometimes inconvenient for human logic and for those who want to 'control' God. Not forgetting that the *Logos* for us Christians is not only a 'word' or a 'book' but, in Jesus Christ, is a 'person' who, through the human encounter, continues the process of disclosure initiated by God since the creation.

Endnotes

[1] John Paul II, Address of His Holiness to the participants in the Plenary Assembly of the Pontifical Council for Interreligious Dialogue. Hall of Popes, Vatican City Friday, 24 November 1995.

[2] *Nostra Aetate* 1.

[3] Pontifical Council for Interreligious Dialogue & Congregation for the Evangelization of the People, *Dialogue and Proclamation, Reflection And Orientations On Interreligious Dialogue And The Proclamation Of The Gospel Of Jesus Christ*, Rome 1991, n. 42.

[4] It is necessary to distinguish the philosophical orientation between the individual and the person. Christian theology contributed to the development of the idea of '*person*', modulating its meaning in reference to the *being* of God and human being, self-awareness and a dimension of "historicity". The very essence of the person, and his/her diversity, is right in his/her relationship with God.

[5] Cf. A. Bongiovanni et al., *Interfaith Spirituality. The Power of Confluence*, (Delhi: ISPCK), 2014.

[6] John Paul II, *op. cit.*.

[7] *Ibid.*

[8] Cf. A. Bongiovanni, *op.cit.*

[9] For an earlier version of the same aspect in Italian, see, A. Bongiovanni, "La Misericordia: categoria chiave del dialogo interreligioso", in Dossier sulla Misericordia, Vita Pastorale, Periodici S. Paolo, Alba (CN), January 2016.

[10] John Paul II, Encyclical letter, *Dives in Misericordia*, Vatican City 1980, n. 1.

[11] The meaning of the Glorious Qur'ān, translated by Muhammad Marmaduke Pickthall, Kitab Bhavan, New Delhi.

[12] Daniel Aruchaparambil, Induismo. Religione e Filosofia, Urbaniana University Press, Vatican City 1996, 249-257.

Spirituality of Dialogue: Pilgrimages in Popular Hinduism

Anil D'Almeida SJ

One of the great discoveries of our century has been the insight of essential interdependence of nations, cultures and groups. The insight has advanced through various forms of contact, exchange and exploration among the various religious traditions. *Nostra Aetate* (Vatican II declaration on Relationship of the Church with Non-Christian Religions) has been a great breakthrough in the positive understanding of other religions by the Church. The document exhorts "all her sons and daughters to recognize preserve and promote all the good things that are found in these ancient religious traditions" (NA 2). In order to dialogue with the other cultures and religions spirituality is needed. In India, "Spirituality is *asādhana* or a religious quest for realization of human's ultimate destiny."[1] In the Indian Church scenario of Inter religious dialogue, due to the missionary and orientalist influences much attention was paid primarily to the Classical Sanskrit traditions and Hinduism was reduced to a version of Classical Hinduism.[2] As a result, in dialogue overwhelmingly the textual study of Hinduism was emphasized. However, the various 'streams' of religious activity and identity loosely connected under Hinduism cannot be equated with Sanskritic tradition. There is a need to look towards the religion of the people to understand the inner dynamism of Hinduism. So, among the Hindus at a popular level in the rural villages, in the fields, along the roads and jungle paths, on the hills and passes, there is a reminder of an invisible world and sacredness. A 'foreigner' could hardly make any distinction between these sacred stones, groves, religious rituals and practices. As pilgrims there is a need to discover the spirituality of dialogue at a popular level.

Hinduism as 'two stream' Religion

Hinduism as a religion of over half a billion Indians comprises a wide diversity of spiritual, theological and cultural traditions. Wendy Doniger in her book *"The Hindus – An Alternative History"* uses the image of the man in the moon that is also a rabbit in the moon, or the duck that is also a rabbit as a metaphor to explain about the complexity of Hinduism.[3] Jawaharlal Nehru, the first prime minister of Independent India, gave an inclusive definition, saying Hinduism is 'all things to all men.'[4] However, today Hinduism is growing as a transnational world religion alongside Christianity, Buddhism and Islam and has developed into a global Hinduism due to yoga, gurus and bhakti cults. On the other hand, a fragmentation which identifies Hinduism with narrowly conceived national identity (*Hindutva*) is destroying the diversity of Hinduism. Along with the classical traditions, the popular religiousness of the people finds expression in many stories, myths and symbols than texts. It is this latter type of religiosity that expresses the yearnings, hopes and struggles of the people. Unlike the religiosity of the Sanskrit classical tradition the polytheistic religiosity is very much centered on and revolves around the material needs of life.

The separation between the classical and popular is always incomplete. Both the classical and popular coexist in a real symbiosis and are linked to each other. So, one cannot easily deny that in spite of divergence of cults and traditions it includes, there is in Hinduism a family similarity. M.N. Srinivas in his book *"Religion and Society among the Coorg of South India"* introduces Sanskritic Hinduism which transcends provincial barriers and is common to the whole of India (1965: 75). Even the Sanskrit tradition simultaneously absorbs and transforms the popular traditions and that process is called desification or laukification (from Loka = People). For example, the local gods take on the name of gods in Sanskrit texts; Murukkan becomes Skanda, Yellama becomes Renuka. In a way, it could be considered as 'cross fertilization.'[5]

Hindu rituals occur at home, in the temple, at wayside shrines, at place of pilgrimages, under trees or in the confluence of sacred rivers called *sangam*. They occur to mark special occasions, to ask for blessings or to propitiate gods and goddesses. The ritual behaviours can be diverse. There are no encoded ritual manuals among the popular practitioner of Hinduism.[6] It is transmitted (*sampradāna*) through oral tradition (*sampradāya*) and it tries to give a shape and degree of unity among the Hindu traditions. For it is in the villages that traditions are born, preserved and transmitted. The rituals are connected with the myths and narratives that give coherence in the ritual celebrations. The narrative traditions provide people with meaning and understanding of who they are and how they came to be as they are. The ritual actions anchor people in a sense of deeper identity and belonging. Many rituals may seem meaningless, but they are seldom abandoned. The goal of annual festivals called '*utsava*' is to propitiate goddess, to avert epidemics and to reduce the attacks of evil spirit as the gods and goddesses of popular Hinduism are not consistently benevolent and they can wield their power to harm people.

Hinduism exists as a living religion, lived out among the common people. Hence, visitors to India are struck by the innumerable wayside shrines to local goddesses or divinized ancestors, majestic temples, garlanded pictures of gods and goddesses in buses, shops and homes, the colour, sounds and smells and vibrancy of daily ritual observances, and by the centrality of religion in people's lives. Among the rituals, pilgrimages to a holy place are common to both the classical and popular traditions and they give a sense of identity to Hindus. Thus, any dialogue that is firmly rooted in the experience of the ordinary masses and popular traditions would reflect deeply the religious world of the religion and would offer spirituality for a genuine dialogue.

Experience (*Anubhava*)

Spirituality involves personal experience (*anubhava*). *Anubhava* is an experience that gets through (*anu-bhu*) and transforms one's life. For religious person any action (*āchāra*) and discourse (*vichāra*) must flow from the experience (*anubhava*) to enjoy legitimacy. In order to draw out the spirituality of dialogue from pilgrimages let me illustrate the experience of going on a pilgrimage to Haridwar-Hrishikesh. I have been to Haridwar and Hrishikesh, the holy pilgrimage centres of Hindus, six times. The first visit was part of studies in the Department of Sanskrit in the year 2004. It was a pilgrimage along with my Brahmin classmate and teachers. After joining the faculty of Vidyajyoti as part of the course on 'popular Hinduism' I accompany students to have *'darśan'* of Gangamā in Haridwar and Hrishikesh. Every visit fascinates and inspires me to go deeper into the understanding of Hindus. The students who have made this *yātra* in a limited way are able to appreciate the devotion (*bhakti*), faith (*Śrāddha*) of Hindus. Sitting on the banks of the holy River Gangā, at Harkipaudi (Foot prints of Lord Śiva) where people believed nectar (*amṛit*) fell and joining thousands in paying homage to the life giving mother Gangā, I am convinced of the fact that a great majority of the people in India especially the ordinary Hindu desires to experience the sacred by going to popular places of religiosity. A longing to be one with is fulfilled by pilgrimages with extraordinary fervour and penance. It's an inner journey, *amārga* in search of their ultimate destiny.

Pilgrimages (*Tīrtha Yātra*)

Pilgrimage is a dominant element of the expressed religiosity of people in almost all religions. In institutionalized religion mechanical ritualistic tendencies lose the charisma, sense of sacred whereas the pilgrimages as popular practice draw people closer to God. Countless Hindus, at some time or other in their lives set out to worship the gods/goddesses in holy places. The holy place can be either a mountain or a river. The places related to mountain are called as *Kṣetras* and river related places as *Tīrthas*. Since, the pilgrimages are compared to Vedic sacrifices in its benefits and are accessible to all, various motives such as purification of sins, fulfilment of a vow, wish for a son prompts Hindus to visit the sacred places. Above all it is to have the *darśan* being in the presence of the deity to attain some kind of identification with the sacred order and to receive *prasāda* – taking part in the leftovers (*uchista*) form the offerings to the deity. The peregrinating instinct is alive among the Indian masses and today the communication era has improved ordinary people's knowledge about Hinduism's sacred centres leading to popular pilgrimages.

A pilgrimage is classically *Tīrthayātra*, a journey to a holy place. *Tīrtha* refers to a 'ford', a place for crossing over. *Yātra* is a movement from one place to another. The movement is a collective ritual carrying people closer to God through a physical movement, which explicitly symbolises the devotees' progress towards unity with the divine. It is believed that supreme becomes concretized in space and time through the images and festivals and his grace becomes localized at the *tīrthas* forever, intensified at sometimes and but always available to the pilgrims.[7] These Pilgrimage places are not made by human arrangements but are divine manifestations. The prominent *yātras* include Kāśīyātra, MānasaSarovarYātra, AmarnāthYātra, PandarpuraYātra, ChārdhāmYātra, Śabarimāla and so on. There are also many pilgrimage centres in different parts of India; some are pan-Hindu like city of Vāraṇāsi or temple of Kanyākumāri. The holy cities on the Ganges – especially Benares, Prayag at its confluence (*sangam*) with the Yamuna and mythical Sarasvati, and Haridwār on its upper reaches are major pilgrimage centres. The Kumbh Mela held every twelve years at different *sangams* attracts vast number of pilgrims. Some Hindus take up 'ChārDhamYātra'- the pilgrimage to all four centres in a clockwise direction to attain salvation.

Symbolism of *Tīrtha*

The *Tīrthas* located on the riverbanks of great rivers have geographical understanding of 'ford'. As pilgrimage places these rivers become symbolic and spiritual fords where one crosses the flood of *samsāra* (cycle of rebirth and death) to attain *mokṣa.*

Tīrtha is also a point of mediation between two realms where the divine world meets the human world, the higher realm meets the lower and the sacred meets every day. As a link between the divine and the human worlds, in every pilgrimage centre deities are commonly present. In a way in the pilgrimage places the invisible, transcendent deity has been 'proven' to be accessible to the pilgrims.

Each pilgrimage centre contributes to 'sacred geography'– For example Kṛṣṇa's homeland of Braj, and Savadatti Yallamma hill (Karnataka) - each centre may be the site of a particular event considered as deity's distinctive manifestation. Thus, the entire land of India from the Himalayas in the north to the tip of India at Kanyākumāri in the south is considered as sacred.

Visiting a pilgrimage centre indicates the journey within oneself.

Various Features of a Pilgrimage

Pilgrimages have certain fixed days of preparation, marked by a lifestyle of more than ordinary penance and fervour, prescribed rites for setting out, the actual pilgrimage, rites at the place, gathering of relics or religious souvenirs, journey home and reception sharing with the neighbourhood, who partially take part in the benefits of the pilgrim. Fasting, worship of deity particularly Ganeśa, continence, prescribed mode of clothing, tonsure before or after pilgrimage is still common. Walking (*pādayātra*) is regarded as most desirable mode on a pilgrimage since merit accrues depending on the nature of the strains experienced. Among all these the great importance is given to *Saṇkalpa*, the explicit declaration of intention to undertake a pilgrimage to a certain place. Along with it the idea of Hindu pilgrim as a temporary renouncer, who walks with only the bare necessities of life, is prominent. Devotionalism (*bhakti*) strongly colours pilgrimage in popular Hinduism. In choosing not to go alone, people partly express the devotionalist idea. The devotionalism is strongly experienced in the Pandharpur pilgrimage to Vittobha, the popular god of the Varkaripanth (pilgrims path) consisting of '*dindi*' (walking groups) in Maharashtra. It was inspired by the writings of Jnāneśvar (1271-96) and Nāmdev (1270-1350). The common pilgrimages enhance the ordinary person's appreciation of Hindu cultural and religious unity.

River Pilgrimage to *Ganga Mā*

ŚatapathaBrāhmaṇa says "In the water, O lord is your seat" (I.1-9). Water is considered as the first element and foundation of the universe. Thus, the river pilgrimage is probably the most popular form of pilgrimage in India. Mother Gangā is the first among India's holy rivers. Till she reaches Bay of Bengal, she flows through many famous Tīrthas such as Gangotri, Gaumukh, Haridwar, Prayāgand Kāśi. *Deva bhūti* (flowing from heaven), *Mandākini* (gently flowing), *Bhāgīrathi* (brought down by Bhagīratha) are among the cult-titles of the hallowed river. Vandana Mātāji living on the banks of Gangā in Rishikesh acknowledges the river to the Hindus as '*mātā*.'[8] Gangā travels as Brahma's companion, flows from the foot of Viṣṇu and is regarded as co-wife with Pārvati to Siva. The Gangā water is regarded as divine energy flowing through the earth cleansing the humans. It enriches and irrigates the soil all along in the gangetic region. She carries an immense cultural and religious meaning for Hindus of every region and every sectarian persuasion.

The utterance of her name is supposed to cleanse the sinner. Pilgrims carry small bottles of Gangā water home to use it on many occasions, even years later, it is supposed to be fresh and unspoiled. The water of Gangā is regarded as elixir, giving immortality if taken in daily. "He who bathes in Ganges purifies seven descendants. As long as the bones of wo/man touch Ganges water, so long that man is magnified in heaven" (Mahābhārata III.85.90). Dying on the banks or even in the waters of the river is heaven. Thus, cremation on the banks or immersion of ashes in the Ganges brings the same benefit. During the pilgrimage immersion of the ashes is one of the objectives of pilgrims. The importance of the cleansing power of Ganga makes it sacred. Gangā water is used as charm to dispel evil spirits and drops are dipped into the mouth of the dying. For the newlyweds; Gangā water is sprinkled over the bride and bridegroom to assure all found wellbeing.

The Gangā especially, is the river of India, beloved of her people, around which is intertwined her racial memories, her hopes and fears, her songs of triumph, her victories and her defeats. She has been a symbol of India's age long culture of civilization, ever changing ever flowing and yet is the same Gangā.[9]

Spirituality of Dialogue Offered by Hindu Pilgrimage

Genuine search for God (Darśan)

The history of India could be seen as a tension between Liberal-Humanist- Śramaṇic[10] traditions with the Conservative-Exclusive-Brahmanic traditions. The tension was to have access to God. The subaltern Hindus were denied access to temple indicating the denial of access to God. The Bhakti tradition of the mid-centuries democratised access to God. In the Bhagavad

Gita Arjuna tells Kṛṣṇa *"dṛiṣṭumicchāmiterūpamaiśvaryam"* (I want to see your divine form" (11:3). This expresses longing of the Hindus in general for the vision (*darśan*) of the divine reality. *Darśan* means 'seeing'. In the ritual tradition of Hindus, it refers to a religious seeing, or the visual perception of the sacred. Even when the Hindus travel on pilgrimages it is for *darśan* of the place or for *darśan* of its famous deities. (eg: Śivas sacred place–city of Benares). Ordinary masses climb up to the top of the mountain for a *darśan* of a well-known local goddess. In the Hindu understanding the deity is present in the image through the *prāṇapratiṣṭā* - transforming *mūrti* (idol) into *vigraha* (dwelling place)-ceremony. Hindu pilgrims are not sight seers but sacred sight seers. We can conclude that for Hindus, pilgrimage is the natural extension of the desire for the *darśan* of the divine image, which is heart of all temple worship. Hindus also value the *darśan* of the holy persons, such as *Sants, Sādhus* (holy men) and Sannyāsis (renouncers). In the villages these holy men are considered as a living symbol of renunciation and a perpetual pilgrim.

Eyes play a prominent role in '*darśan*'. According to the *Śilpa Shāstras* (knowledge of Architecture), when the divine image is to be made the eyes are the final part of the anthropomorphic image to be carved. The divine images are often striking for their large and conspicuous eyes. Indian popular art represents the God with big eyes inviting the bhaktas to meet the enormous eyes of God, to see God, to have a *darśan*. Having *darśan* is to worship God. [11]Agehananada Bharati in his book 'The Ochre Robe' writes, "There is absolutely no parallel to the conception of *darśan* in any religious act in the west." [12]

Graciousness of God (kṛpā)

Popularly while visiting any pilgrimage centres, Hindus use the expression in Hindi '*darśandena*' (give darśan) or '*darśanlena*' (take darśan). It means that an act of '*darśan*' is not initiated by the worshipper; rather, the deity presents itself to be seen to his devotee. As sacred perception, to see the divine image is given to the individual as a gift (*prasāda*). Arjuna is given the divine eyes (*divyachakṣu*) to see *Kṛṣṇa* in the theophany described in the Bhagavad Gītā.[13] To see and to be seen by the deity is considered the grace of God. Through the eyes one gains the blessings of the divine.[14] One of the terms used for grace is *Katākṣa*. It means looked at with a side glance or side look, a leer. It is a word borrowed from love literature meaning a side glance. The divinity is compared to a lover that cannot avoid throwing side glances at the beloved. God's glance is salvific.[15] When a Hindu visits a pilgrimage centre, he or she yearns for the glance of the deity to obtain grace. Thus, the desire for grace can be seen in every Hindu, especially during the *Kumbh Mela*, in spite of water being muddy and the pūjā material strewn all around people still do not mind immersing themselves in it for they believe it is *amṛit* or nectar.

Sacredness of Everything

The sky in the pot is measurable, sky in the sky is immeasurable, but through the sky in the pot one is in touch with the sky in the sky (*ghatākāśa*). This is a criterion Indian minds habitually uses. To be in touch with the sacred, Yogis and Sādhus and Sannyāsis and the like turn inward. The great majority of people seek the same outside of them, in sacred places, objects, persons, considered as privileged centres for special manifestations of the divine (*amśavātara*). In a pilgrimage centre ordinary people see sacredness in water, mountain, river, holy men and women, transforming the whole place as "sacred geography," filling everything with awe and wonder '*Mysterium Tremendum Et fascinats.*' It shows the aspiration of ordinary Hindus to be in touch with the divine. The Divine is one but it manifests in different forms. The Kaṇha Upaniṣad says "just as fire though one, having entered the world assumes separate forms in respect of different shapes, similarly the Self inside all beings, though one, assumes a form in respect of each shape; and yet it is outside."[16] In all these devotions and looking everything as sacred, the love of nature, and intimate knowledge of the hills, seashore and fields is evident that inspires the devotees not only to love the particular deity but also the landscape where he or she lives. Therefore, the sacred groves (*bana*) are protected as part of religious custom.

Spirituality that Makes Use of All the Senses
When a devotee visits a pilgrimage centre or any temple, he or she makes full use of the senses - seeing, touching, smelling, tasting and hearing. A visit to Holy River Ganga comprises seeing Ganga, touching it by sprinkling the water on body (*sparṣa*) or bathing, listening to the sacred mantra or myth (*śravana*) related to Ganga Mātha, sipping of sacred *gangājal* or the consecrated food during *Gangāārati/pūjā*. It also involves the ringing of the bells, offering of oil lamps, the presentation of flowers, the pouring of water and milk and so on. In all this popular Hinduism celebrates the life of this world and realms of the senses, to establish the presence of the divine deity within them. The challenge is to interpret through hermeneutics not from the classical forms created by various religious traditions, but in the ordinary images of people's traditions, rites, and daily activities.

Spirituality using Narrative/images/symbols

Hindu spirituality is often portrayed as interior, mystical and other worldly. But this one-sided characterization of Hinduism is from a classical perspective. The symbols, narratives, rituals performed in the pilgrimage places are not based upon abstract interior truths, but upon the concrete and particular appearances of the divine in the substance of the material world. In the temples we also see portrayals of myths and legends. There are *tirthas* which are primarily connected to the particular image of the deity. There is a close relationship between the image and pilgrimage.[17] Pilgrims going to the sacred hill of Tirupathi in Andhra Pradesh and the Varakari sect oriented toward the *darśan* of a particular deity Viṭhobha in Mahārāshtra, and the wooden images of Kṛṣṇa Jagannāth, Balarām and Subhadra in the great temple complex at Puri are image oriented pilgrim centres. India's myths are living in the geography of the land and conversely India's geography is alive with mythology.[18] The land of Kurukṣetra, the site of Great War of the Mahābhārata, the land of Kṛṣṇa called Vraja are some examples. Even in Christian tradition the sites where Mary nursed Jesus, the place where Mary washed Jesus' clothes and the place where food was cooked to be served at the last supper, were located with imaginative perception. Pope Gregory I had recognized the didactic value of images: "for that which a written document is to those who can read, that a picture is to the unlettered who look at it. Even the unlearned see in that what course they ought to follow; even those who do not know the alphabet can read there."[19]

Spirituality of Social Significance

The inward looking and rather individualist religiosity of Hinduism offers healthy socio-cultural correctives in the pilgrimage. Pilgrimages provide opportunities for people of different traditions (*sampradāyas*) to meet each other and experience some amount of community feeling. It contributes to a certain degree social cohesion and feeling of togetherness in spite of rigid caste system and restrictions of ritual purity–pollution. They also become occasion for socio-cultural interactions and widening of perceptions. This broadens and deepens the Indian perspective which Hinduism is trying to evolve i.e. pan-Indian Hinduism. Wider diffusion of religious belief and practices takes place, while spending time and listening to Gurus/Sādhus in various *Akhādas* and *Aśrams*. It also leads to revival and renewal of Hinduism.

Rishikesh – Haridwar pilgrimage opened the windows of my heart to see the richness of Hindu tradition and wealth of wisdom. The very fact that most of us are comfortable being with the ordinary Hindus indicates that we share the same heritage with them. Practices of Catholic pilgrimages resonate with the popular Hindu pilgrimage traditions. Can we reform and recover the dimension of pilgrimages in our own traditions calling for integral spirituality that meets the inner aspirations of people? We have a call to form ourselves as inter religious person. The spirituality offered by the pilgrimage would help us for a better dialogue and it calls for a radical attitudinal changes. According to Catherine Corneille, to practice genuine inter-religious dialogue, one needs doctrinal or epistemic humility to accept one's own fallibility and imperfection, commitment to a particular religious tradition, interconnection to find out meeting points and empathy or hospitality to the authentic truth of the other.[20] Hospitality is a basic ethos of Indians. As co-pilgrims of the divine we need to move from hostility to hospitality for a better dialogue.

Endnotes

[1] Michael Amaladoss, "Indigenous Theology and Spirituality of Action," *VJTR 40/2* (February, 1976), 74.

[2] Felix Wilfred, "Christianity in Hindu Polytheistic Structural Mould: Popular religiosity and the Hindu –Christian Interaction", Archives de Sciences Sociales des Religions 103, 1998, 75.

[3] Wendy Doniger, *The Hindus: An Alternative History*, (New York: Penguin Press, 2009), 1.

[4] Quoted in B.K. Smith, "Exorcising the Transcendent: Strategies for Redefining Hinduism and Religion" in *History of Religions* (Aug 1987), 36.

[5] Wendy Doniger, *The Hindus: An Alternative History*, 6.

[6] The BrāhmaGa texts are considered as liturgical texts of Hinduism.

[7] Klaus K. Klostermaier, A *Survey of Hinduism*, (Albany: State University of New York Press, 1989), 312.

[8] VandanaMataji, *Living with Hindus*, (Delhi: ISPCK,1999), 16.

[9] Diana L. Eck, *Banaras: City of Lights* Routledge & Kegan Paul, London 1983, 215.

[10] *ŚramaGa* meaning ascetic: Buddhism and Jainism are considered as *śramanic* religions as they opposed ritualistic tradition of Vedic times.

[11] George Gispert- Sauch, *Gems from India,* (Delhi: ISPCK/Views, 2006), 102.

[12] Agehananda Bharat, *The Ochre Robe* (New York: Doubleday and Co., 1970), 161.

[13] Bhagavad Gītā 11:8

[14] Diana L. Eck, *Darsan, Seeing the Divine Image in India,* (New York: Columbia University Press,1998), 3.

[15] George Gispert-Sauch, "Grace in the Viścmādvaita tradition," in *Divine Grace and Human Response,* ed., C.M.Vadakkekara, Ashirvanam, Bangalore 1981, 34.

[16] *agnīryathaekobhuvanampravicto, rūpamrūpampratirūpobabhuva, eksaśthathasarvabhūtāntarātmarūpamrūpampratirūpobahischa,* Kama Upanishad. II. 9.

[17] Victor and Edith Turner, *Image and Pilgrimage in Christian Culture* (New York: Columbia University Press, 1978), 15.

[18] Diana L. Eck, *Darśan: Seeing the Divine Image in India*, 69.

[19] Cited in Albert C. Moore, *Iconography of Religions, An Introduction*, (Philadelphia: Fortress Press,1977), 243.

[20] Catherine Cornille, *The impossibility of Interreligious Dialogue*, (New York: A Herder & Herder Book, 2008), 4-5.

Spirituality of Dialogue: Qur'anic Perspective

Shaheena Khatib

A vision capable of sustaining the efforts to promote good and harmonious relations between the followers of different religions makes sense of "Spirituality of Dialogue".

It constitutes a natural meeting point for the followers of different religious traditions and fruitful efforts for interreligious dialogue. It is an essential and crowning form of dialogue between men and women of different religious experiences. It enables persons rooted in their religious traditions, to share their spiritual riches.

It may be a source of mutual enrichment and a stimulus towards fruitful cooperation for promoting and preserving the highest values and spiritual ideals of humanity. Within this dialogue there will be ample opportunities for "the reason for hope".

The spirituality of dialogue can be used as a tool to elevate human conditions to a plane on which the mind is focused on higher purpose of pure life, a reality of peaceful co-existence.

The final testament Al- Qur'ān provides common grounds for the peaceful co-existence of diverse religious communities in Chapter 49 verse 13

> "O men! Behold, WE have created you all out of a male and a female, and have made you into nations and tribes, so that you might come to know one another. Verily, the noblest of you in the sight of ALLAH is the one who is most deeply conscious of HIM. Behold, ALLAH is all-knowing, all-aware."

This concept provides a key that could open the door to interfaith dialogue. The Qur'an embraces cultural & social pluralism emphasising that equality in regard to biology and dignity is common for all people. Therefore, nobody has an inherent superiority over others. Prophet Mohammad (BPUH) announced:

> "No Arab is superior to a Non-Arab and no white person is superior to black person."[1]

Diversity in fact is the most beautiful sign of our unity. It has been mentioned in the Holy Qur'ān.

> "And among his wonders are the creation of the heavens and the earth, and the diversity of your tongues and colours: for in this, behold, there are messages indeed for all who are possessed of (innate) knowledge!" (30,22)

It indicates the harmonious co-existence of diverse religious communities and protects the rights and freedom of the followers of all religions. Qur'ān indicates the reality of diversity of humanity. So, it is clear that peaceful co-existence is an essential requirement of all human beings on this world.

Peace is the most fundamental value in the final testament. It invites everyone to enter whole heartedly into peace (submission to creator Chapter 2, verse 208).

"O you who have attained to faith! Submit yourselves wholly unto ALLAH."

Submission, conciliation, peace-making, safety, security, and assurance of peace overlap with the meaning of Peace in Qur'ān. Demonstrating security is a mark of reliable trustworthiness. The deeper meaning of routine life salutation "Salaam" has a greeting of security-peace.

It is not possible to have a uniformity among human beings of different colours, gender and shapes. Diversity in Nature is a key factor which guides us that every created being has its own species and purpose with some special qualities. Likewise, it is not possible to put the entire humanity on a track of single religion, as it is the choice of every individual.

Freedom of religion has been granted by the Creator himself. He has given the formula for a peaceful coexistence on this planet earth. The study of heavenly scriptures in its original text makes human beings sensible enough to connect their soul to their Creator.

So, why the difference of religion amongst us is not accepted as a natural phenomenon? If our Creator wished such uniformity in religion, it would have been very much possible for HIM to do so. The Divine Wisdom says on this issue in chapter 76 verse 3 after narrating that commonly HE has provided every human being inputs like hearing and vision with common sense to apply with the mind to work and intelligence to decide:

"Verily, WE have shown every human the way: (and it rests with him to prove himself) either denier of facts of this life and life to come or prove himself grateful accepting the realities and act nobly."

But human history has witnessed that majority of human beings does not care about the orders of their Master, their Creator and nowadays all human societies are losing human values of **Purpose, Principle, Process,** and **Protocol.**

- As human beings we must know that our **Purpose** of existence is to submit ourselves to our Creator, with free-will;

- The **Principle** of life is to be fruitful for our fellow beings with humbleness;

- The **Process** is to seek guidance by an in-built "GPS system" (inner self) through Scriptures and connect to your Creator.

- The **Protocol** is "Let the Spirit Lead the Matter" for revitalizing human values through the system of Prophets.

We had a great model of godly persons reflecting noble and honest line of action with a great zeal and zest. I invite all the intellectuals of the society to cooperate each other for peaceful coexistence on this planet Earth because we all belong to the same race: HUMANITY.

Endnotes
[1] *Hadith*, «Last Sermon of the Prophet Muhammad», MUSNAD AHMED 22978.

Spirituality of Dialogue: A Buddhist Perspective

Dechen Dorjee

We have an important topic on the table today. The fact that we are here to contemplate and willing to understand the significance of genuine dialogue is in itself a milestone in the larger narrative of pluralism, where we are moving from mere diversity to active "energetic engagement with diversity" on all levels of society around the world. We cannot afford to remain as an island and not to have any encounter with other community or faith in this shrinking world. And, if we wish that encounter to be positive, peaceful, harmonious and powerful, there is no other alternative but to understand the other. Although the task at my hand is not easy, and being a human being limited by my own means, I hope I could do justice to this topic.

As we start our discussion, another important thing that I wish to clarify in the beginning is that for this discussion to be genuine and meaningful we have to step beyond the idea of "mere tolerance" and understand the culture of acceptance on the basis of understanding and respect. To understand the other person, the other community or faith, we have to actively seek the information and learn the differences that exist. Tolerance is of course a virtue, but it does not inspire us to learn about the other faith, rather it tends to create a wall between the one who tolerates and one who exercise their faith, thus automatically strengthening the stereotypes. Ignorance, assumptions, fears could possibly stem up from too much tolerance, which we know creates the pattern of violence and division in our society.

In addition, we also have to challenge the sense of superiority or inferiority of one faith over the other, or one community over the other, so that, we meet each other at a level field. Meeting at a level field doesn't mean that, we have to forget our differences, and assimilate. Yes, we are all different, but we have to accept our differences in relationship to one another through genuine understanding. If we as human beings, or representatives of certain faiths, understand ourselves as coming from a tolerant faith, which only for the sake of religious or social harmony, is participating in this dialogue, and otherwise, in our heart holds our faith as the only supreme faith in the world, then we may not be able to create a conducive environment for any sort of dialogue to happen.

Hence, I would like to start from a point where I have genuine respect for all faith traditions as equal and supreme and understand the need of plural faiths in this world given varying human dispositions. My religion is neither superior, nor inferior to any other faith and I am not here to promote any religion as versatile. I am here to listen, contemplate, understand and share my understanding. And, I sincerely hope that we are all on the same page.

Another very important aspect of a meaningful dialogue is its continuity in the long run, where people listen, understand, and engage at varying levels depending upon their capacity and continue the process of dialogue in their life. A spirituality of dialogue for few hours and few days, without any real sense of continuity and engagement wouldn't help much. Hence, I hope the ripples keep forming and we keep engaging in such meaningful dialogues in our own personal and professional capacities.

In the time we live in now, although we call ourselves modern, it has become a real challenge to strike a meaningful dialogue. There is so much noise, chaos, distraction, assumptions, and most of all, a distorted sense of self-importance, over-confidence and defence, that we often find ourselves and people, engaged in monologue, rather than dialogue. Monologue emerge from "I essential", and "my indispensable" attitude that is encouraged in our era through all means like education and media, and we become mere victims to the colossal consumerist design. Consequently, we end up in more conflict and misunderstanding.

However, the solution for all the misunderstandings, problems, conflicts, only lie in education and engaging in meaningful dialogues which could build closeness, and trust, the fundamental values that we miss these days. His Holiness the 14th Dalai Lama says that 21st century is the century of dialogue and inter-religious dialogue is the key to ending violence and terrorism in this world.

That's why today I want to share how we can make meaningful dialogue through Buddhist perspective. Actually, Buddhism is essentially a philosophy of dialogue, debate, and dialectical understanding. When we look at the *Sutras* (discourses), there are only few words uttered by the Buddha himself. The whole sutra is in a form of dialogue and discussion between various participants. For example, in *Prajnaparamita sutra*, there are more than eight participants who are engaged in a discussion within themselves and Buddha intervenes only occasionally. That participatory dialogue speaks to richness of the discourse.

However, rather than getting into the philosophical subtleties of Buddhism, I wish to draw a simple way for us to understand dialogue from a Buddhist perspective of 'Four Noble Truth and the Eight Fold Path', which stand as the primary and basic teachings of Buddhism. They are commonly and widely shared that we sometimes tend to overlook or simplify their values. Therefore, I would like to stick to these ideas and try to explore the richness that is embedded in this seemingly simple thought.

In the Noble Eight Fold path, we have the idea of 'correct speech' or 'right speech' (Skt. *āryāṣṭāṅgamārga*; Tib. འཕགས་པའི་ ལམ་ཡན་ལག་བརྒྱད་པ་, Wyl. *'phags pa'i lam yan lag brgyad pa*) which I often describe as 'mindful speech' or roughly as 'wise speech', (Skt. *samyagvāc*; Tib. ཡང་དག་པའི་ངག་, Wyl. *yang dag pa'i ngag*) is the primary factor in any dialogue or inter-religious dialogue.

According to Buddhism mindful speech has certain qualities that make it different from rest of the speeches. The external quality or the physical form of the speech is devoid of four non-virtuous elements of speech ངག་གི་ཉེས་པ་སྤྱོད་པ་བཞི (Wyl. *ngag gi nyes pa spyod pa bzhi*) Pron.: *ngak gi nyepa chöpa shyi, Skt.* चत्वारि वाग्दु शचरितानि, *catvāri vāgduścaritāni*, *Pron.: chatvari vagduscharitani*. These are 1. Lying, 2. Divisive speech, 3. Harsh speech and 4. Idle gossip (or worthless chatter). These four are external qualities of our speech. However, our speech constantly corresponds with our mind and mental state, where we need to pay attention to the 'three non-virtuous elements of mind, ཡིད་ཀྱི་ཉེས་པ་སྤྱོད་པ་གསུམ། (Wyl. *yid kyi nyes pa spyod pa gsum) Pron.:* yi kyi *nyepa chöpasum Skt.* त्रीणि मनोदुश्चरितानि *trīṇimanoduścaritāni.* We have to make sure that our mental state is devoid of these ailments namely, 1. Covetousness, 2. Ill will (or wishing harm on others) and, 3. Wrong views.

However, all of us clearly know that it is not easy to attain a virtuous mental state to be able to make the mindful dialogues that we so much wish to engage in this world. Hence, it comes out to be of paramount importance for us to clear the barriers of mental afflictions to be able to speak mindfully or wisely. And Buddha, being the wise one, knew that the way to clear our mental dispositions is through genuine realization of problem, acceptance, commitment, and taking steps to change or alleviate the problem. And that according to Buddhism could be done, through the Four Noble Truth: 1. The truth (or reality) of suffering (Tib. སྡུག་བསྔལ་གྱི་བདེན་པ་, Skt. *duḥkha-satya*) which is to be understood, 2. The truth (or reality) of the origin of suffering (Tib. ཀུན་འབྱུང་བའི་བདེན་པ་, Skt. *samudaya-satya*), which is to be abandoned, 3. The truth (or reality) of cessation (Tib. འགོག་པའི་བདེན་པ་, Skt. *nirodha-satya*), which is to be actualized, and 4. The truth (or reality) of the path (Tib. ལམ་གྱི་བདེན་པ་, Skt. *mārga-satya*), which is to be relied upon.

Moreover, to realize and accept the nature of suffering, we have to understand the concept of equality and exchange. In Buddhism we have this concept of empathy and compassion, as opposed to sympathy. In the practice of empathy and compassion, we place ourselves in the place of the other person in pain, and try to understand that pain and generate compassion, whereby we also understand the nature of suffering and pain, and thus come closer to accepting the reality of life.

And attaining the virtuous mind is of course not an instantaneous process. It takes a lot of introspection on self, and intentionally putting into practice the avoidance of non-virtuous deeds through the practice of the Five Paths which falls under the sub-section of the Truth of the Path, and they are: 1. the path of accumulation (Skt. *sambhāramārga*) 2. The path of joining (also called 'engagement' or 'junction') (Skt. *prayogamārga*) 3. The path of seeing (or 'insight') (Skt. *darśanamārga*) 4. The path of meditation (or 'cultivation') (Skt. *bhāvanāmārga*) 5. The path of no-more-learning (Skt. *aśaikṣamārga*)

These five paths incorporate the entire spiritual journey, as described in Buddhism. It is indispensable to follow these five paths from the very beginning till the stage of complete enlightenment. From a broader perspective, these five paths could be applied to every practice that we undertake in our daily life. The first path, the path of accumulation is the stage of understanding, which could be applied, in our case, to attain mindful speech. The second path is the path of joining which is the stage of experience. Here we have to put in practice the accumulated understanding of mindful speech and analyze its benefit. The third path of seeing is the stage of realization. Here we get the clear realization of our mindful speech. The fourth path is the path of meditation or cultivation, where we cultivate the realized mind, which in our case is mindful speech. The fifth path is the path of no more learning where the virtuous mental state becomes an intrinsic part of our nature, and in our case mindful speech becomes a natural way of communication. This is the ideal stage for any dialogue to become substantial.

The final stage is where we engage in meaningful dialogue without any superficial thought, action and speech. I wish to sum up by saying that, in this paper I have only been able to touch on the few basic concepts of Buddhism in relation to dialogue. However, I sincerely wish that we would continue this culture of inter-religious engagements in the future too and keep enriching our diverse community.

Spirituality of Dialogue: Christian and Hindu Perspective

Joseph Satyanand IMS

Sarveṣām svastir bhavatu,/ sarveṣām śāntir bhavatu/ Sarvesām pūrṇam bhavatu,/ sarvesām mangalam bhavatu //

Sarve bhavantu sukhinah,/ sarve santu nirāmayāh / Sarve bhadrāṇi paśyantu, /mā kaścid duhkhabhāg bhavet.//

We live in era of paradoxes. On the one hand there is an increase of secular values like liberty, equality, justice and humanism and on the other hand there is a menacing rise of religious fundamentalism in all the religions. Today some of religious men sponsor terrorism. They also motivate others to a life of fundamentalism and even the use of violence against not only people of other religions but also sects within their own religion. They have a narrow interpretation of their own religious texts. It is a well-known fact that opposing views and claims of the world religions have had led humanity to wage wars against one another and thousands have perished in religious wars and Communal conflicts and riots. Taking the signs of the times seriously Pope Saint John XXIII of happy memory, convened the Vatican II Council. One of the concerns of the Church in modern times is peace in the world. The Church seeks the cooperation of people of good will to establish the Kingdom of God on earth.[1] Vatican Council II has spelled out the relationship of the Church with the people of the world religions. The Catholic Church realizes that Church is not the Kingdom of God but is the sign and the sacrament of God's salvific action in the world. The Church is the servant and the sign of the Kingdom of God[2] and is to work with people of other religions and spirituals traditions for the realization of God's Kingdom.

Inter Religious dialogue is a work of the Holy Spirit

God who created the universe by his word and by the power of his Spirit is at work in human history. Inspiration and the guidance of the Holy Spirit were at work in the convocation and the conduct of the Second Vatican Council (1962- 1965). The Council document on Inter Religious Relationship is known as *Nostra Aetate* (1965). It is the declaration of the Church on her relationship with other faith traditions in appreciation for the presence of the Divine in the world religions. *Nostra Aetate* can be described as the *Magna Carta* of Inter Religious Relationship.[3]

Nostra Aetate marks the beginning of a new era in inter-cultural and inter-religious interactions and international relationships that have been taking place over the years in industry, technology, finance and ideologies. The new phrase 'Global village' is the actual symbol of that process. In the post Vatican II area, the Catholic Church has been taking leadership in bringing people of all faiths and even non faith organizations to serious dialogue and collaboration. Church believes that humanity has one and the same source of origin and has a common destiny. The Second Vatican Ecumenical

Council (1962-1965) has noted that all human beings have the same origin and the same destiny.[4] Making this world a better place for all human beings is a responsibility for all of us. Therefore, the Church promotes sincere dialogue in a spirit of mutual respect to solve all the tensions and conflicts between religions, nations, races and political parties and groups and for the promotion of peace, prosperity and harmonious coexistence. Working together with persons of other Faith traditions to foster fraternity and friendship to advance peace and harmony in this world is one of the most important inspirations from the Second Vatican Ecumenical Council.

We live in a world of plurality of religions, races, cultures, languages, religious and socio-political ideologies and traditions. No one can wish them off. Plurality of religions is a part of God's salvific action in the world. The variety we see in the world is God willed and is to be nurtured and to be cherished. Unless we learn to appreciate our common heritage and respect the differences, we will be agents of hell here on earth[5]. Pluralism is our strength and the differences make us unique, giving each one an identity. Partners in dialogue have to develop a spirituality of inclusive pluralism.[6]

Hinduism

India has been a land of Religious pluralism and cultural diversity for centuries. She has developed a sense of unity and security in the midst of diversity. The Second Vatican Council acknowledges with respect the uniqueness of Hinduism in *Nostra Aetate:*

> "Thus, in Hinduism men explore the divine mystery and express it both in the limitless riches of myth and accurately defined insights of philosophy. They seek release from the trials of the present life

through ascetical practices, profound meditation and recourse to God
in confidence and love". (NA 2).

Among the world religions, Hinduism is the earliest of the living
faiths in the world. Hinduism claim to be the *Sanātana Dharma*,
the eternal or the Universal Religion.[7] Some of the special
characteristics of Hinduism that make it a unique religious
phenomenon or the *Sanātana Dharma* are the following:

Uniqueness of Hinduism

Hinduism has no historical beginning. It has no founder – an
avatāra or a prophet or a saint. Hindus accept, as it is declared in
the Bhagavad Gita, that whenever there is a decline of religion,
God descends (*avatāra*) on earth to re-establish religion and
moral order (*dharma*), to protect the righteous and to destroy
evil.[8] Hinduism accepts many 'descents/manifestations of God'
(*avatāra*).[9]

Hinduism has many sacred books. They belong either to
Śrūti[10] or *Smṛti*.[11] But Hinduism does not impose any one singular
scripture as absolutely authoritative for everyone who wishes
to be a Hindu. *Śrūti* books are known as the Vedas. Among
the *Śrūti* texts, Ādi Śamkarācarya, accepts the *Upaniṣads* (the
philosophical wisdom and experiences of the Vedic sages) alone
as authoritative. The Ritualistic Mīmāmsā schools accept the
Brāhmaṇas (the ritualistic texts dealing with Vedic sacrifices)
alone as authoritative scriptures.

Popular and practical Hinduism is based on the religious
beliefs and values of the *Smṛti* Literature, the *Itihasas, Purāṇa*-s
and the *Āgama-s*. Hinduism has an innate and creative spirit to
invent new types of religious literature according to the needs
of the time without denying or abrogating the scriptures of old.

Belief in God is not central to Hinduism.[12] A Hindu who believes in God is not bound to accept any particular dogmatic affirmation regarding the nature of God. A Hindu may believe in one God (monotheism) or in many gods (polytheism), or a God with a name and a form (*saguṇa, sākāra*) and *bhakti* as a means to attain liberation or an impersonal abstract/pure Absolutism without a name and form (*nirguṇa, nirākāra*), who is realised through *jñāna*. In Hinduism new gods are recognised or accepted whenever required while the fortunes of many of the Hindu gods have changed, some have risen in glory (e.g. *Kṛṣṇa*) and some have lost their popularity (e.g Indra). Hinduism also does not insist on any defined dogma that has to be accepted by everyone, including the most fundamental doctrines of *karma* and rebirth (*samsāra*). A Hindu is born Hindu and does not cease to be Hindu unless publically denounced it.

Similarly, Hinduism does not impose any particular religious rituals or any one specific moral code (*Dharma Śāstras*) and sacraments (*samskāras*) as obligatory to all the Hindus equally. They are subject to change and substitution according to the demands of the times. In all these matters Hinduism has been exceedingly tolerant and magnanimous. There is no one centralised authority to regulate the Hindu way of life. Therefore, it could sponsor new scriptures, new gods, new *avatāras,* new institutions, new philosophies and doctrines according to the needs of the people. In Hinduism no dogma is defined as binding on the followers. In fact, all the contrary and contradictory doctrines are reconcilable within the larger perspective of Hinduism.[13] They are different ways or glasses through which one looks at the same reality. The Reality is One, but perspectives are different. This is the right attitude for a meaningful and enriching interreligious dialogue.

Hinduism has capacity for almost infinite expansion

Hinduism the most ancient religion is ever vibrant because of its capacity for integrating and absorbing everything good and special it comes in contact with. The Vedic Āryans did not destroy anything of value of the conquered people, contrary to the practice elsewhere in the past, but integrated them into their list of gods, rituals, cultural practices and social structures. The ability to absorb and to integrate makes Hinduism in possession of a unique capacity for almost infinite expansion.

Hinduism: A Conglomeration of Religions

Hinduism is not a single religion, but only a common name given to a unique religious phenomenon emerging from the conglomeration and amalgamation of many religions, belief systems, gods and their mythologies and rites that have ever existed in India from the prehistoric times to our own days.[14] One may compare Hinduism to the mighty river Ganges, into which many other major tributary rivers from distant places flow in, bringing along with them huge amount of water of many other minor and major sub tributaries, all of them contributing to the making of the river Ganges. Hinduism can also be considered as a beautiful garden, but not planned. In this garden there are many trees, some big and mighty, some small but beautiful, some bushes and a variety of flowers each finding a space for itself in the garden. Hinduism has not only survived but also flourished through centuries in spite of the many onslaughts on it from the invading powers.[15]

With its glorious experiences of the past, Hinduism can play a great role not only for the peaceful coexistence of religions but also to build a better world for all.

Religions

Each religion is unique. Religion is embodied in the particular culture of its origin. Often this culture determines its rituals and celebrations. Religions born and developed in a particular geographical area carry with them the baggage of the culture of their origin in their forms of worship, the prescriptions and regulations concerning human conduct and interpersonal and intrapersonal relationships.[16] Religion develops sacred rites, symbols, signs and sacred formulas (liturgy/*karma kāṇda*) to celebrate the mysteries of its religious experiences and laws to protect its structures.

Religion tends to get institutionalized

Religion tends to get organised and institutionalised with specified sacred books, dogmas, rituals, ceremonies and code of conduct. When religion gets structurally organised and institutionalised, it is bound to ascribe certain infallibility and absolute authority not only to its scriptures but also to religious structures and religious laws that are developed and organised around it in the course of time. These are officially imposed. The institutionalization brings about, on the one hand, a certain amount of coherence and unity among its followers. But on the other, it excludes others from the blessings and fruits of its religious experiences and spiritual attainments as stated in the '*extra ecclesiam nulla salus*' statement.

Religion is widely accused of being one of the primary causes of division and hostility in communities and nations all over the world. Religions have often become isolating and divisive, communal and sectarian to the extent of rivalry/ aggressive hostility/exclusivism. What is more deplorable is the tendency to consider others who do not belong to their fold as enemies/pagans, *Kafirs* and *mlecchas* to be conquered or even to be destroyed. Holy wars and terrorism in the name of religion are results of such an exclusivist attitude. These are aberrations and abuses of religion. This has caused hatred resulting in great sufferings, wars, bloodshed, and loss of lives and property.

Suspicions and estrangements of the past keep the religions apart even today. Ignorance of one another's religion and an attitude of cultural and religious superiority and triumphalism could create in us a sense of suspicion and intolerance at others' presence in our domain. How can religions cooperate among themselves and work for fraternity and friendship when there are so many differences among them? We need a change of attitude. *Nostra Aetate* calls for such a change of attitude. A change in our attitude can come only through a process of self-criticism and self-renewal.

Religion and Spirituality

Religions have to undergo a process of self-analysis and self-criticism and stress their essence, namely the unique spirituality they possess. What is common to all religions is that they are a means to spirituality. However, there is a distinction between religion and spirituality. Since religiosity is expressed through elements of the particular culture, it is quite clear why tensions and conflicts take place. Spirituality, on the other hand, can have resonance with other similar spiritualities without tension or conflict. Spirituality is generally understood as a unique quality of the soul that can transcend the physical realm. Although the essence of Spirituality is more in 'being' than in 'doing' our actions manifest our inner being/spirituality. Spirituality influences our attitude towards and responses to the reality of our context. Spirituality affects our vision for life, our value system and relationships. Religion, as a medium of spirituality, can be considered to be the best of human organisations. Spirituality is the essence and the spirit of religion.[17] No religion is absolute, only God is absolute[18]. Such knowledge should make us less smug in the practice of our own religion, more respectful of other denominations and religions, and more willing to let God's vision triumph over ours.

The Path ahead is Dialogue

Our concepts of the important elements of faith are influenced by many factors. Some of the most important elements that determine our understanding of God, soul and human destiny are culture, sacred scriptures,[19] belief systems, worldviews, and religious traditions. They are the coloured glasses through which we look at reality. They have mutual influence and they determine the quality and the character of faith, theology, spirituality and religious praxis. As our ancient sages declared, 'Reality is one, but the philosophers describe it differently.'[20] These differences are mainly due to our finitude and limitations. This ability to see the One Reality differently is not only to be respected but also to be nurtured.

It is a fact that religions differ in their concepts of God. There is substantial difference in the understanding of meaning and the means of salvation in various religions. These concepts influence behaviour of religious people. Inspite of these genuine differences the only way forward to lasting peace and development in this world is the path of dialogue in all openness and humility. Dialogue is the only means to solve conflicts even in our families, in our country and in the universe. An exclusivist or even a pluralistic attitude does not demand a dialogue. A pluralistic attitude may recognise and tolerate the other as another way. But a dialogical attitude will transform and enrich the partners with the riches of one another.

The historical document *Nostra Aetate* marked a Copernican revolution in the attitude of the Church towards the world religions by opening her doors wide for dialogue and cooperation with all people of good will by removing misunderstandings, prejudices and elements of hatred.[21] On the whole, a global perception of cooperation is evolving steadily. As in other sectors, so in the religious sector too, it is a transitional phase. Creative interaction among religions and cultures has become a necessity. It is ultimately a definite step towards truth in its myriad forms of manifestation. Hence there is every reason for establishing creative bond with the world of faith, whether it is Christian, Hindu, Muslim, tribal/indigenous or any other.

The present Holy Father, Pope Francis gives great importance to interreligious dialogue. It is evident from his Apostolic Exhortation called '*Evangelii Gaudium* '(The Joy of the Gospel).[22] He emphasizes the importance of dialogue with civil society, the state, science and other cultures. He describes dialogue as a necessary condition for peace in the world and is a duty for Christians as well as other religious communities to promote dialogue with an attitude of openness in truth and love in spite of various obstacles and difficulties especially forms of fundamentalism in their respective religions. The only way to lasting peace in the world is an honest dialogue. Pope Francis led the heads of the warring states of Israel and the Palestine through their respective President Shimon Peres and Mahmoud Abbas to pray together at Vatican on 8 June 2014 for mutual understanding and peace.

Religions as Families

Religions are to be understood as families having certain common beliefs and values special to the family. Religious family has its own language and communication systems. Some of these families of religions are deeply rooted in the culture of its place of origin. These can be better understood only when one gets into that family. Without getting into the culture and the worldview of the family, one cannot grasp its culture, communication and the value system. Scriptures, dogmas, rituals and ceremonies are all meaningful within the family and for the members of the family. They cannot be imposed on others - the neighbouring families.

Each Religion, culture, race, language has its own uniqueness. They must have their space to exist, to develop, to function and to contribute their mite to the totality of the human family. One family cannot claim to be superior to the other family. Such claims have disastrous consequences for everyone.

We must look at humanity as one family. Another human person, even if he does not belong to our family, to our religion, to our country, is not an enemy to be avoided/killed. All human beings are intimately related to one another. A genuine inter-religious dialogue reveals to the participants that no human being can ever be a stranger. We all belong to one family or *Vasudhaiva kudumbakam* (वसुधैव कुटुम्बकम्)[23] as taught by ancient sages.

The teachings of Jesus emphasise the unity and oneness of humanity. He taught us that God is our Father and we are brothers and sisters (cf. The Sermon on the Mount in Mathew Chapters 5-7). God loves all people. The parable of the Wedding

Feast clearly indicates that all are invited to share in the glory of heaven.[24] Jesus has made it clear that in his Father's house there is a place for everyone.[25]

Religions as the colours of the Rainbow

We could consider each religion in the world as one of the shades that contribute to the making of a beautiful rainbow. Absence of any of the rays/colours diminishes the beauty of the rainbow.

All the religions have their own unique understanding of God. What is common in every religion worth its rational foundation is that it holds the Supreme Reality (God) as ineffable, beyond all human imagination, conceptualisation, and language. Everything we think and describe about God, even our scriptures and dogmas, are all finite and inadequate. They are all partial expressions of the Reality. The finite human intellect cannot grasp totally the Infinite Reality. Of course, we can grasp the truth but our understanding of the truth is limited on this side of eternity. Our ancient *Rṣis* experienced it when they declared '*yato vāco nivarttante aprāpya manasā saha. Ānandam Brahmaṇṇo vidvān na vibheti kadacana eti*' (Tait. 2.4).[26] We are limited and finite beings. God is the Infinite and the Absolute being. None of us at any time can grasp/ understand the absolute and infinite God completely with our finite and limited mind/intellect. God does not change, but our understanding of God can change. We can always grow in our understanding of the mystery of God.

Identity and Difference

Inter-religious dialogue has not yet reached at any consensus on many theological issues. This remains as a hurdle because there are differences between religions. Differences are as real as what is common to all religions. In fact, there is an identity and there are differences between various religions. This reality of identity and difference is called *bhedābhedavāda* in Indian tradition. But what is primary is identity. Are identity and difference equally important? What is substantial is identity and what makes each religion unique is the difference. Difference gives each religion its own identity. Our identity is in and through and because of the difference. Therefore, both identity and difference are important. Let us celebrate everywhere and always what unites us and what is common to us. This must be the first priority for everyone.

The differences are equally important. These make each religion unique. While celebrating what is common and what unites us let us also open our eyes to what is special to the religion of our neighbour. Let us also celebrate the uniqueness of each religion. Celebrating the uniqueness of others, if taken correctly, does not lead us into relativism and the naïve belief that all religions are equal. Such openness to the other will help us to realise our own uniqueness - our specific differences from others.

Peace and harmony are important values

In spite of our differences we have to work together for peace and harmony in the world. Peace and harmony are the gifts of spirituality and any religion worth its name must strive to be agents of peace and harmony in this world religious faith tradition. Our life must witness our spirituality and the uniqueness of our religion through service to our neighbours. This is what Jesus has asked his disciples - to be his witnesses to the ends of the earth.[27]

While celebrating our uniqueness, let us not forget that God is love and he loves all people, all are precious to him, because he is not a God of a few - the reigning deity of a tribe. God is the Lord of the Universe. God's salvific intent is universal. God desires the salvation of all people of all religions, races and nationalities. Jesus has correctly said he has 'other sheep' who are not of this fold. "Then people will come from east and west, from north and south, and will eat in the Kingdom of God" (Luke 13.29). God's love and revelation embrace everyone.

Church's contribution to dialogue in India

Christianity in India is as ancient as Christianity itself. Tradition has it that India received the Gospel of Jesus Christ from St. Thomas, one of the twelve Apostles of Jesus Christ, who arrived on the shores of Kerala in 52 A.D. and suffered martyrdom on 3 July 72 A.D. at Mylapore in Chennai. The remnants of the Communities of faith that St. Thomas raised up in Kerala are known as St. Thomas Christians or Syrian Christians, who have given us a glorious tradition of patriotism, peaceful coexistence, collaboration and nation building.

Foreign missionaries who came to India during the days of the colonization have done a lot of work to foster fraternity and friendship for peace and harmony by promoting vernacular languages and uplift of the poor. Who among the Hindi scholars can forget Rev. William Carey and Fr. Camil Bulke or who among the social workers can ignore Mother Teresa of Kolkata? The colonizers introduced modern education, administrative set-ups, modern communications and transportations and rule of law based on equality, liberty, justice and fraternity. They also contributed to the development of all vernacular languages of India and even Sanskrit. The first grammar book and even the first dictionary in most of the Indian languages were written by missionaries. These were all attempts at promoting dialogue and fostering fraternity and friendship as understood by them in their context. After 2000 years of existence in India, the Christian community forms hardly 2.5 per cent of Indian population. Following the lead of Vatican II, the Church in India understands herself as a co-pilgrim with all people of good will, moving towards the Kingdom of God. The Church as a pilgrim has been moving away from its restricted mono-religious perception of Medieval times to its current self-understanding of being the sign and the sacrament of the Kingdom of God. Therefore, the Catholic Church in India invites all people of goodwill, of all religions and ideologies to work together to create a new world of cooperation and transformation for the Kingdom of God'.

The Christian community in India is a tiny one, yet it takes care of at least 25 percent of all charity works, schools of education and centres of primary health and hygiene in India. All the services of the Church are made available to the poorest of the poor and the most neglected children of Mother India in the most remote villages and forests of India where no one else either of the Government or of other religions dares to reach out to. When the country is struck by natural calamities like earthquakes in Gujarat and Latur, tsunami in Tamil Nadu, cyclone in Andhra, floods in Uttarakhand and recently in Jammu and Kashmir, or anywhere else in the country, the Christian community is always there with its generous help. The mere fact that the Christian community still forms hardly 2.5 per cent of the Indian population proves that proselytizing has never been a major trust of the Church's missionary activity in this country.[28] After Second Vatican Council, more than ever, one of the primary concerns of the Catholic Church in India has been to work hand in hand with people of all religions in fostering fraternity and friendship among the people by building bridges of friendship and cooperation as emphasized by the National Seminar in Bengaluru in 1969.[29] As part of our nation building let us build bridges that unite us and not walls that separate us.

Commission for Interreligious Dialogue

The Catholic Bishops' Conference of India (CBCI) has clearly marked out the path of triple dialogue for the Church in India: dialogue with the poor, dialogue with the culture and dialogue with religions of India. Fostering collaboration and friendship with all people of good will is a way of life for the Church. For this purpose, the CBCI has set up a Commission for Interreligious Dialogue, which was initially headed by Bishop Patrick Paul D'Souza of Varanasi.[30] He set the tone and the spirit of the CBCI Commission for Interreligious dialogue in India. He guided the Church in India on the path to dialogue with people of all religions.

The Church in India has contributed greatly to the building up of mutual trust and collaboration among people of various religions, ideologies and races. This thrust of the CBCI has been encouraged and blessed by the Holy Father St. John Paul II.[31] Quoting the CBCI document on 'the role of the Church for a better India' (8 March 2013), Pope Francis points out (cf. *Evangelii Gaudium*, no 250) that interreligious dialogue can begin with a conversation about human existence or simply being open to people of other religions by sharing their joys and sorrows. Dialogue is possible only when there is an attitude of love and concern for others.

Dialogue and harmony in Varanasi

The tiny Christian Community in Varanasi is actively involved in the promotion of dialogue and cooperation among various communities. The first ever Interreligious Live Together programme was organised in Varanasi in 1975. The initiative was taken by Bishop Patrick D'Souza of Varanasi. At that time, he was the Chairman of CBCI Commission for Interreligious Dialogue and the Secretary was Fr. Albert Nambiarparambil CMI. They organised such live programmes for people of various religions in different parts of the country.

Our thrust is harmony

The primary thrust of all the services of the Church in Varanasi is to build harmony, peace and development of the people. This thrust is manifested in all the schools, health care centres, social development projects, and small saving schemes for women and the village poor that the Catholic Church undertakes in Varanasi. The formation programme that we give to those who are going to consecrate their lives as Priests and Religious in this part of the country is fully permeated by the spirit of interreligious dialogue and collaboration.

Almost all the Catholic institutions in Varanasi have different programmes aimed at promoting brotherhood and fellowship among people of different religions and cultures. All schools celebrate not only the national days but also important feasts like Deepavali. The Bishop's House invites all the Muslims friends for an *Iftar* meal during the month of Ramzan. *Iftar* meals are also arranged by some of our centres and institutions like Maitri Bhavan, Asmita and Vishwa Jyoti Communications. Christmas Milan and Holi Milan are also part of our celebrations. Interreligious prayer meetings are conducted in many of our centres of service. Matridham Ashram invites Gurus, Sadhus and Maulvis for its annual Satsangh in November. Nav Sadhana Kala Kendra is a university college founded by Bishop Patrick D'Souza for the promotion of Indian music, dance and folk arts and culture. Such a college is rare in this part of north India. In the context of fostering harmony and peace two of our institutions need special mention. They are Maitri Bhavan and Jan Sanchar Samiti.

Maitri Bhavan

Maitri Bhavan or Friendship Home in Varanasi is well known to the journalists and the intellectuals of Varanasi as a real home of love and fellowship. Maitri Bhavan is an early initiative of the Church to promote interreligious relationship and cooperation.[32] Maitri Bhavan has been a model for celebrating diversity of faith and fostering love and peace. Various activities that Maitri Bhavan renders to promote communal harmony and collaboration among various religious and ethnic groups in Varanasi are the following:

a. Interreligious prayer

b. Celebration of festivals of all religions

c. Seminars on world religions

d. Seminars on cultures and civilizations

e. Seminar on various Scriptures

f. Seminar on current issues

g. Bringing people together and working actively for promoting peace and harmony among the people of all religions

h. Conducting training programmes in interreligious dialogue for the religious and students of various educational institutes of the country as well as from abroad.

Maitri Bhavan also collaborates in conflict management and peace building processes initiated by people of other faiths as well as other institutions and universities in the city of Varanasi and elsewhere.

Vishwa Jyoti Jan Sanchar Samiti

Vishwa Jyoti Jan Sanchar Samiti was established by the IMS Fathers for social and spiritual transformation of people through low cost media. Some of the activities of the Vishwha Jyoti Communications of Jan Sanchar Samiti are the following:

a. Prerna Kala Manch gives awareness and inspiration on pluralism and diversity of religions through stage dramas, street plays and songs. It also organises dramas against communalism, prejudices and biases, apart from making appeals.

b. Shanti Yatras all over north India for religious dialogue, peace and harmony.

c. Tyagarchana Shanti Yatra was conducted together with Swami Saccidananada Bharati of Nagpur in 2015 to all the towns of UP promoting peace and harmony among people of all religions.

d. Celebration of feasts of all religions under the banner of 'Kashi Qaumi Ekta Manch' (Forum for Kashi's Communal Harmony). Kavi Sammelan and Mushayara are part of these celebrations. There is no doctrinal discourse, but only sharing of joy.

e. Dialogue in Action: Taking imitative to join hands with people of all religions to be at the service of the poor and the suffering during natural calamities like flood, cold wave and also at the time of riots (Gujarat riots in 2002).

Peace and harmony through service

All the institutions that the Catholic Church has in Varanasi aim at fostering fraternity and friendship with people of all religions. The cause of peace and harmony in the country is a priority for all the institutions and the personnel of the Church in Varanasi. We are committed to:

– Cultivating a friendly, welcoming and healthy relationship with all our neighbours irrespective of their religious affiliations. It is very important to begin a dialogue of life with our immediate neighbours. A dialogue of life can be initiated by visiting the neighbours regularly, taking part in their celebrations, and also in theirs joys and sorrows.

– Coming closer to the situation of the people and getting involved in the life struggles of the poor for survival irrespective their religious, ethnic and linguistic affiliations. The poor have a preferential priority in all our services.

– Being open to share the resources and facilities of our institutions with our neighbours, who are our immediate partners in interreligious dialogue. Our neighbours are helped to feel and experience that we are there for them. Their concerns and life struggles are matters of our own concern. We invite all people of good will to join us and to work together for the creation of a better world in our own locality. Some of our institutions organise seminars and awareness programmes like literacy, healthcare, social realities, terminal illnesses like AIDS, and counselling.

- Having different forums to interact with different groups of people like religious leaders, intellectuals, politicians, civil servants, youth and women. The discussions and deliberations in these forums are meant to promote communal harmony and people's development. These forums will network with like-minded agencies and GOs and NGOs.

- Celebrating important national days like Independence Day/Republic Day/Gandhi Jayanti/Mahila Diwas/Bal Diwas; and feasts like Deepavali, Raksha Bandhan and Harvest Festivals in common with the local people of all castes and creeds. Making use of such occasions to create an attitude of appreciation for the common heritage of all people and strengthening bonds of fellowship for interreligious cooperation and communal harmony and national integration. We strengthen these bonds by inviting people of other faiths to take part in our celebrations and feast like Christmas and join their celebrations. This helps us remove fears and suspicions others have about us.

- Taking initiative to form religious harmony groups in our locality for organising periodically seminars and academic and intellectual get-together for people of various religions. Courses and study programmes on the religious beliefs and spiritual experiences of people of other faiths will create an attitude of openness to their spiritual experiences. Conducting interreligious prayer meetings for common issues and concerns of the people will also promote communal harmony.

- Praying together for peace/harmony/special needs is a powerful means of building bonds among people and communities. The historical world day of prayer for peace organised by St. John Paul II at Assisi on 27 October 1986 or the prayer together hosted by Pope Francis for warring Israeli President Shimon Peres and Palestinian leader Mahmud Abbas at Vatican on 8 June 2014. We organise such prayer meetings on special occasions like communal tensions, natural calamities like earthquake and floods.

– Organising live in programmes for all faiths. Such programmes give opportunities to share deeper religious experiences and remove most of the prejudices among the participants. At the level of God experience, most of our prejudices and fears are removed. This is true even in the case of atheists who are open to some type of absolute values beyond themselves.

– Making it possible the study of other religions in our schools and colleges. We also have to impart general knowledge of other religions at various levels of education. We have to introduce the learning of the sacred books of other religions, their Bhakti literature, and Sufi saints in the academic programme.

– Respecting the religious sensibilities of the people, their religious practices, their temples and gods, and their scriptures. For centuries God has been making use of these symbols to grant them his graces and blessings.11. Getting experts trained for interreligious dialogue and relationships. We need to be tolerant towards the pioneers and their attempt at building interreligious fellowship and cooperation.

Conclusion

Plurality is the key to understanding India. This must be kept in mind in our interactions with people of other religions. We have to develop an open mind. The infinite can be expressed in infinite ways.

Other religions are not the fortresses of the enemy. They are the temple of God experiences for people other than us. As temples they are to be entered with utmost respect. As Christians we believe that the Holy Spirit is at work in human history. The Vatican II has opened our eyes and minds to the fact that Holy Spirit is at work beyond the boundaries of the Church and the Hierarchy. The Catholic Church promotes and advances the cause of interreligious harmony and peaceful co-existence and takes leadership in bringing people of all faith to work together to create a better world for everyone here on earth.

Hinduism has always welcomed whatever is *satyam śivam* and *sundaram*. India is not only the cradle of many world religions, she has always welcomed others. Zorastrianism, Christianity and Islam came to India and flourished here. India has taught the world as how to live with people of different cultures, languages and religions could live in peace and harmony and contribute together to the building of the Nation. Dialogical cooperation is a prophetic mission of our times so that together with our dialogue partners, listening to the voice of the Spirit, we steadily move towards the Kingdom of God joining our prayers with the wish of the Upanisadic sage: With the sage let us pray,

Aum saha nāv avatu saha nau bhunaktu, saha vīryam karvāvahai,

tejasvī nāvadhītam astu mā vidviṣāvahai. Om śāntih! śāntih! śāntih!'

'Om! May both of us be protected; may we be nourished; may we work together with great vigour; may our learning be illumined. Let there be no animosity between us. Om Peace, Peace, Peace'.

Endnotes

[1] The Vatican Council has reflected on various issues and concerns of the Church and of the mankind. Through various documents the Church has earmarked the path she intends to take in the realization of the Kingdom of God in our times. The self-awareness of the Church is reflected in the Dogmatic Constitution *Lumen Gentium* (1964). Church's awareness and her Pastoral role in the modern world are described in a document known as *Gaudium et Spes* (1965).

[2] In the past the Church had taught and held the view that outside the Church there is no Salvation (*extra ecclesiam nulla salus*).

[3] The document declares "For all peoples comprise a single community, and have a single origin, since God made the whole human race of men dwell over the entire face of the earth. One also is their final goal: God, His providence, His manifestations of goodness" (NA 1).

[4] All men form but one community. This is so because all stem from the one stock which God created to people the entire earth (cf. Acts 17.26), and also because all share in a common destiny, namely God. His providence, evident goodness, and saving designs extend to all men (cf. Wis. 8.1, Acts 14.17, Rom 2. 6-7, 1 Tim. 2.4) against the day when the elect are gathered together in holy city which is illumed by the glory of God, and in whose splendour all people will walk (cf. Apoc. 21.23ff). (*Nostra Aetate* n.1).

[5] This is what the ISIS is doing in Iraq and Boko Haram in Nigeria and the 'Cow protectors' in India.

[6] By Inclusive Pluralism I mean that I cannot exclude the other (partner/ religion) from my vision of reality. The existence of the other can no longer be on peripheral of my faith. I must also respect the differences as part of the reality. The differences are something unique to be promoted.

[7] Perhaps the first encounter of Jesus Christ with Hinduism might have taken place at visit of the wise men from the East (cf. Mt. 2.1) to the manger of the new born child Jesus in Bethlehem. It is reasonable to assume that these wise men from the East were from India, the land of Arya Bhatta (476-550 BC) and the Vedic Astrologers.

[8] Bhagavadgītā 4.7-8

Yadā yadā   hi dharmasya glānir bhavati Bhārata/   abhyutthānam adharmasya tadātmānam sṛjāmy aham// ParitrāGāya sādhūnām vināśāya ca duckṛtām/ dharma samsthāpan'ārthāya sambhavāmi yuge yuge//

[9] It is incorrect to translate the term avatāra as incarnation. Avatāra means descent, coming down of God. Hinduism accepts many avatāra-s even in animal forms. Incarnation is a Christological term. *Caro* in Latin means flesh and Incarnation means the Word (Logos) becoming Flesh and dwelling among us (cf. Jn. 1: 14). In the Christological context there is only one Incarnation - the person of Jesus Christ.

[10] The Vedas are the *Śrūti*. The Vedas eternally exist. They are *apauruseya* and are uncreated. They were originally handed down orally and therefore are known as *Śrūti* (what is heard).

[11] The post-Vedic religious texts of Hinduism go by the common appellation of *Smṛti* literature. *Smṛti* means memory. Hinduism produced new religious books starting with the Vedas down through *Itihāsa-s* (Epics) to the *Purāṇa-s* (legends) and the *Āgama-s* (Sectarian writing) as the need arose. The *Smṛti* literatures, especially the *Purāṇa-s* are like a shelf in a library, wherein new additions are placed as the need arises.

[12] Many of the Hindu orthodox philosophical schools of Hinduism (e.g., the *Sāmkhya, Vaiśecika* and *Mīmāmsā*) do not accept the existence of a Supreme God.

[13] *Indram mitram varunam agnjimahu ekam sadvipra bahudha vadanti (Rg Veda 1.164.46)*

[14] The main streams that contributed to the cultural, spiritual and religious wealth of Hinduism are, *Vedism* (Brāhmaṇism of the Vedas), the elements of the religions that later emerged as *Vaiṣṇavism, Śaivism and Śāktism*. Hinduism is a conglomeration of at least these four religions. In fact, these religions in themselves are amalgamations of many minor and major religious traditions, rites, and practices having different objects of worship (gods) and mythologies. This process, which we call today as a process of inculturation, had in fact effected, on one hand, the 'brahmanization' of the non-Vedic religions and cultures as well as their worldviews, and, on the other hand, contextualization and inculturation of the Vedic Brāhmaṇism.

[15] It is a great achievement compared to what has happened to Christianity in the Middle East, Egypt, Turkey, etc.

[16] The doctrines, rituals and structures of organized religions can be better understood in their context - historical, cultural, social, geographical, climatic and material conditions like the availability of (the kind of) food, the sources of livelihood, etc. Mythology, religious rites, concepts and descriptions of gods, etc. differ from culture to culture.

[17] A truly spiritual person slowly recognizes the limits of his culture and gradually distances himself to some extent from even his own traditions and cultural limitations because he realizes that Truth/Reality can be viewed from different angles.

[18] Although some religious men may think that God s under their custody, God cannot be caged.

[19] A fundamentalistic approach to any sacred scriptures is dangerous. It generates arrogance and crusades. Simply quoting the texts from one's scriptures is not enough to prove religious doctrines to others, much less scientific theories. As far as the Holy Bible is concerned the commentaries of the ancient fathers and the findings of modern scientific scholarship are important and help to understand the literary genres, the historical, cultural and theological backgrounds of the text.

[20] *Ekam sad vipra bahudha vadanti*

[21] The theology of grace and the role of other religions in the economy of salvation have made us to be more open to the working of the Holy Spirit in the world. Recognition of the working of Divine Grace beyond the known boundaries of the official Church and the role of other faith traditions (*Nostra Aetate*, 2) in the economy of salvation have far reaching consequence for the Church. That is the reason the Catholic Church has created after the Second Vatican Council a new Department in the Vatican which is known as the Pontifical Council for Interreligious dialogue, which deals with Church's relationship with the World Religions.

[22] See Nos. 250-258 of the Apostolic Exhortation of Pope Francis, Evangelii Gaudium, published on 24 November, 2013.

[23] Vasudhaiva Kutumbakam ('vasudhā,' means the earth; *'ēva'* means indeed; and *'kutumbakam'* means family) is a Sanskrit phrase which means "the world is one family". The original text reads, ' *Ayaṁ bandhurayaṁ nēti gaṇanā laghucētasām | udāracaritānām tu vasudhaiva kumumbakam ||* It means that the discrimination saying "this one is a relative; this other one is a stranger" is for the mean-minded. For those who're known as magnanimous, the entire world constitutes but a family. (Cf. Panchatantra V.3.37, 3rd C. B. C), Hitopadśe a 1.3.71 (12tt.C. AD). This generally is understood as referring to need for the entire humanity to live together as a family in perfect peace and harmony.

[24] Mt. 22. 1-14. Through this parable Jesus teaches that all are invited to the Kingdom. 'Go therefore into the main streets, and invite everyone you find to the wedding banquet.' Those slaves went out into the streets and

gathered all whom they found, both good and bad, so the wedding hall was filled with guests (Mt. 22.9-10). See also the parable of the dragnet (Mt. 13. 47-48).

[25] Jn. 14.2. 'In my Father's house there are many dwelling places. If it were not so, would I have told you that I go to prepare a place for you'.

[26] Whence words return along with the mind, not attaining it, he who knows that bliss of Brahman fears not at any time (Tait. 2.4). Jesus said to the Samaritan woman, 'woman believe me, the hour is coming, when you will worship the Father neither on this mountain nor in Jerusalem. You worship what you do not know; we worship what we know, for salvation is from the Jews. But the hour is coming, and is now here, when the true worshippers will worship the Father in spirit and truth, for the Father seeks such as these to worship him, God is spirit , and those who worship him must worship in Spirit and Truth' (Jn. 4.21-24).

[27] Acts 1.8. 'And you shall be my witnesses in Jerusalem, in all Judea and Samaria, and to the ends of the earth.'

[28] People who do not want the poor to be helped, cared for or educated accuse the Church of attempting to convert the poor through her services to humanity. That it is a false accusation is clear from the fact that even after 2000 years of her existence and services in India Christians form only 2.5% of Indian population.

[29] The Conference of the Catholic Bishops of India (CBCI) meeting at Calcutta in 1974 restated the same vision in these words "In view of the fact that India has nurtured several of the world's great religions the Church in India is called upon to be an earnest pioneer of interreligious dialogue. It is the response of Christian faith to God's saving presence in other religious traditions and expression of the firm hope of their fulfilment in Christ" (CBCI Calcutta 1974, p.140).

[30] This Commission has brought out a document in 1989 titled "Guidelines for interreligious Dialogue". It explains the nature and the content of interreligious dialogue. While explaining the meaning of interreligious dialogue the document considers Inter religious dialogue as "both an attitude and an activity of committed followers of various religions who agree to meet and accept one another and work together for common ideals in an atmosphere of mutual respect and trust" (No.31).

[31] Pope John Paul II has specially pointed this out to the Bishops of India, on 1st Feb. 1986 at New Delhi, in the following words "Another matter that occupies your zeal is interreligious dialogue. This too is

serious part of your apostolic ministry. The Lord calls you, especially in the particular circumstance in which you are placed, to do everything possible to promote this dialogue according to the commitment of the Church". The Pope expressed similar views when he visited Delhi again in November (6-8), 1999.

[32] Maitri bhavan in Varanasi was founded by Fr. Ignatius Puthiadam SJ and Fr. Neeti Bhai IMS, with due permission of their respective religious Superior and the local Bishop in 1981. Initially it functioned at a rented house in Ravindrapuri Extension, later it moved to Nagwa (1985). It has been relocated to Bhelupura in 1996 at the initiative of Bishop Patrick D' Souza.

Spirituality of Dialogue:
A Christian – Muslim Perspective

Anand Mathew IMS

In the recent times, the world experiences a turmoil of cultural and religious conflicts. Therefore, this seminar on Inter-faith dialogue has a greater relevance. In the context of fierce attacks and violence by IS terrorists, some say that there be no dialogue with Islam, and some are demanding more and more dialogue. On July 2016, a prominent Catholic social activist from Kanpur appealed to Pope Francis to organise a dialogue with Islam along with leaders of other faiths. I do not consider myself academically capable of speaking on this delicate issue. At the same time with your blessings I am making a humble yet diffident attempt to understand the spirituality of Dialogue especially in relation to Islam.

Some Experiments and Some Experiences

In the year 2000, Advocate Surendra Charan, a renowned Christian of Varanasi and I founded Kashi Qaumi Ekta Manch (KQEM, Forum for Communal Harmony in Kashi). We started organising inter-faith celebrations. We decided not to have doctrinal discussions, but only celebrations. Feasts like Diwali, Holi, Hanuman Jayanti, Buddh Jayanti, Ambedkar Jayanti, Eid-ul-Fitr, Eid-ul-Zuha, Guru Nanak Jayanti, Guru Govind Singh Jayanti, Ravidas Jayanti, Christmas and Easter were celebrated with each other. People of diverse religions conveyed festal wishes to each other through songs and other cultural programs formally and informally. *Kavya goshthi* or poets reciting self-composed poems on communal harmony and other social issues were regular features of these celebrations. I cannot claim that these meetings were regular. But for the past 14 years, we have been regular in organising *Roza-Iftar*, breaking of the fast during the holy Ramzan month, in our centre. People of all faiths and Muslims in large numbers participated. This took a new turn six years ago, when we shifted the venue and focussed on organising *Roza-Iftar* for the *rozedar* (fasting Muslims) convicts in the central jail, Varanasi. The positive aspect of this program is that it is being organised in collaboration with Muslims, Hindus, Sikhs and Christians.

Micheal Amaladoss speaks of four types of dialogue, viz: Dialogue of Living, Dialogue of Reflections, Dialogue of Spiritual Experience and Dialogue of Action. In India, we cannot escape from the dialogue of living, because we live in an inter-faith atmosphere. Dialogue of reflections takes place in our dialogue centres. Dialogue of spiritual experience may be rare and much more need to be done in this sphere. We in Varanasi have been involved in a dialogue of action. KQEM has also undertaken activities which are of 'Dialogue of/in Action' nature. Relief activities during flood, cold wave, relief to the victims of Gujarat carnage, relief to the flood victims from Kashmir who took refuge in Varanasi are some of the activities.

The inter-faith celebrations, *Roza-iftar* and Dialogue in Action activities have given us opportunity to come closer to the people of other faiths and Muslims in particular.

Lahore Experience

From 11th to 14th Sept. 2006, I had the opportunity to visit Lahore as part of a delegation from India of the Indo-Pak Friendship Forum. While in Lahore, one morning as I woke up, my friend Faisal from Delhi showed me the headlines of the day printed in big letters in Urdu condemning Pope Benedict's statement made on the previous day (September 12) in Regensburg University. The Pope had quoted a 14th-century Byzantine emperor who said, "Show me what Muhammad brought that was new, and there you will find things only evil and inhuman, such as his command to spread by the sword the faith he preached." The Pope did not originally dissociate himself from the citation, and the media quoted it out of context. Then Muslims in various parts of the world responded violently, killing Christians and burning churches. I realized that tension was building up in Lahore and there was resentment all around. Next day we had to wait two hours to get permission to enter into the Lahore Catholic Cathedral compound for a visit. Because of the threats issued by extremist elements, there was a huge police force guarding all the churches in Pakistan.

At the same time, we met Muslims who were understanding and large-hearted. On the same evening, along with some of the Indian delegates and Pakistani friends, I also had to deliver a speech in a meeting organised in a prestigious hotel. The elite of the Lahore city, mostly Muslims, were present. I was neither aware of the full context of Pope's statement, nor the exact quote. I only knew that something had gone wrong. So, I apologized on behalf of the Christian community and as an 'antidote' I based my talk on Mt.5:9, *"Mubarakvaad unhe, jo melmilaap karaate hain. Ve khuda ke aulaad kahlaayenge."* (Blessed are the peacemakers, for they shall be called sons of God). People appreciated the talk and many of them personally came to me after the program and we had a meaningful interaction discussing in detail on the need of dialogue.

The next day we were in the Lahore market. While sipping tea in a wayside *dhaba,* in the midst of general conversation, some customers in the shop realized that we are outsiders from India. Immediately they stood up from their seats and extended their arms to embrace us. While in their arms a few of them whispered into my ears, words of genuine love and welcome. This experience has increased my love and respect for Muslims. On the one hand, there are threats issued by the extremist groups and extra precautions of safety by the administration, but on the other hand there are arms extended with genuine love.

Can we Dialogue with Islam?

Apart from my personal experiences, the question often heard in the Christian circles is "Can we dialogue with Muslims?" Christianity and Islam together represent more than half of the world's population. With a heavy baggage of some negative experiences, and also prejudices and biases which are results of these negative experiences, and unfortunately generalisations and stereotyping, members of each community blame the other side for conflicts, both ancient and contemporary. Dialogue, however, presents us with an opportunity to hear Muslim concerns and express our own—such as our desire for greater religious freedom. And dialogue can lead to results.

Although there were many violent incidents in different parts of the world after Pope Benedict's statement in Regensburg, there were Muslims who called for dialogue. A group of 38 Muslim scholars from around the world tried to bring the encounter back to the academy through an open letter to the pope. The Muslims who signed the open letter include grand muftis who are authorized to make legal decisions for Muslims in their countries. Other signatories are professors at major universities in the Muslim world and the West who influence the rising generation of Muslims. The opportunity to engage with them is significant.

Notwithstanding the ugly headlines, attention to Benedict's speech and the events that led up to it can aid productive dialogue between Muslims and Christians. And the stakes could not be higher.[1] These moderate leaders are contending for the soul of Islam. By responding thoughtfully to their letter, we can reflect the words of the Biblical prophets to "seek the peace of the city to which you have been taken"—and the words of Jesus, who said, "Blessed are the peacemakers." Christians need to try to see issues from the vantage point of these Muslim leaders and respectfully allow them to define their own faith. In so doing, we will commend our faith—and our Savior—to them.

The Holy Qur'ān actually affirms the Holy Bible. Prophet Muhammad granted Christians liberty to conduct services in the city of Najran.

Muslim Scholar's Response to Pope Benedict XVI

The 38 Muslim leaders took respectful issue with several of the Pope's points, drawing attention to what they called "errors" in the Regensburg lecture.

Suggesting that Islam is tolerant only when tactically necessary, Benedict attributed the qur'anic verse, "There is no compulsion in religion" (2:256), to the first period of Muhammad's ministry, when he "was still powerless and under threat." The Muslim scholars, however, said that reliable qur'anic commentaries place the saying in Muhammad's second period, when Muslims were in a position of strength. Indeed, it is important to look at the historical context (what Muslims call "the occasion of revelation") when interpreting qur'anic passages. In this light, we need to recognize that many of the peaceful references do indeed come from Muhammad's earlier period, when he was primarily preaching a message that had parallels to the biblical prophets. His latter period, however, involved a message that was combined with political and military power.

The Muslim scholars took issue with the charge that early Muslims spread the faith by the sword. Yes, they acknowledged that political Islam spread partly via conquest. But they believe the greatest part of Islam's expansion came from Muslim missionaries.

The scholars also noted that the Muslim duty of jihad, often called "holy war" in the West, refers to "struggle in the way of God"—which can take many forms besides war. Then they listed some historic Muslim legal guidelines concerning warfare that are similar to the historic Christian Just War theory. We need to remember that although our Lord said, "Love your enemies," his followers have often resorted to the sword instead of the Cross. It's no surprise that many Muslims interpret the present Western military involvement in Afghanistan and Iraq as a Christian crusade.

The scholars also took issue with the Pope's description of God in Islam as absolutely transcendent. They called this characterization a misleading simplification that fails to note Muslims' belief in God's immanence, which they said is clearly communicated in the qur'anic assertion that God is closer to a person "than his jugular vein." They also said the pontiff erred in citing a marginal Muslim theologian to support his position.

Citing the Islamic theologian *Ibn Hazm*, Benedict XVI suggested that Muslims believe God is not bound by such human categories as reason. The Muslim scholars in turn noted the many discussions on the relationship between faith and reason in the history of Islam. What Christians should remember is that many of the theological questions Christians have debated – such as the relationship between faith and works or divine sovereignty and free will – Muslims have debated, too. While there are clearly theological differences between Christians and Muslims, it might surprise some to know that the Muslim word for God, Allah, is the same term that Christian Arabs used long before Muhammad – and still use today. Further, the attributes ascribed to Allah – including love – closely track those ascribed to God by Jews and Christians. This is not to deny that Muslims reject other fundamental Christian understandings – especially God's self-revelation in Jesus.

The letter also recognized religious values common to Muslims and Christians. Likewise, it approvingly quoted the Pope's statement in Cologne on August 20, 2006: "Interreligious and intercultural dialogue between Christians and Muslims cannot be reduced to an optional extra. It is, in fact, a vital necessity, on which in large measure our future depends."

The Muslim scholars added: "It seems to us that a great part of the object of interreligious dialogue is to strive to listen to and consider the actual voices of those we are dialoguing with." This element is important for all Christians, not just Roman Catholics.[2] In fact, both Muslim and Christian scriptures enjoin that we not only be peacemakers, but that we also bear respectful witness of our faith:

- "If they incline toward peace, then you should incline" (Qur'ān 8:61).

- "As far as it depends on you, live at peace with everyone" (Rom. 12:18).

- "Invite to the way of your Lord with wisdom and good admonition" (Qur'ān 16:125).

- "Always be prepared to give an answer to everyone who asks you to give the reason for the hope that you have. But do this with gentleness and respect" (1 Peter 3:15).

Holy Qur'ān Advocates Harmony of all Religions

As per Holy Qur'ān, the oneness of humanity is applicable to people of all faiths, despite differences in faith. All are equal before Allah because Allah is the Sustainer of all – *Rabbal-Alamin*, even of unbelievers. True unity in Islam should not encounter any barrier – ethnic, racial, territorial or religious.[3] The Holy Qur'ān desires that pluralism is respected and diversity is maintained and throws a challenge to the believers to live in peace and harmony despite differences of faith:

> To every one of you we have ordained a law and a way, and had God so willed, He would have made you all a single community, but He did not so will, in order that He might try you by what He has given you Vie, then, with one another on doing good works, to God you

shall all return; then He will make clear to you about what you have
been disputing (5:48).

Qur'ān also wants the believers not to abuse others' religions
or gods as it does not serve any purpose, it directs the Muslims
not to argue on matters of faith:

> Believers argue only in the best way with the people of the Book, (but
> contend not all) with such of them as are unjust. Say, "We believe in
> what has been revealed to you; our God and your God are one; and
> to Him we submit." (29:46)

Qur'ān has many verses which as the believers of the Book
(Jews, Christians and Muslims) not to fight on theological
dogmas (e.g. 2:112). Asghar Ali says that theological dogmas
which are man-made, and which reflect egos lead to conflicts.
We should not allow these to rule over us and divide our
humanity.[4] Truly, a free human being who believes in being a
spiritual person, should transcend these dogmas, and instead
should follow the directives of the Word of God and build a
society, which respects religious diversity and plurality.

Islam and its Willingness for Cultural Adaptability

In spite of the teachings of Qur'ān to respect other religions,
the non-Muslims seem to be prejudiced. Muslims are often
blamed for their unwillingness to adapt the culture of the place.
There are allegations on the Muslims that they do not adapt the
local dress, language of worship, eating habits and other small
and big aspects of day to day living which in fact make up the
social culture. There are different perspectives to these issues.
My personal experience in Varanasi is that a large number of
the Muslims in Varanasi had adapted the local culture and they
are deep-rooted in the Varanasi culture. In our country, and
especially in Varanasi, the cultural capital of India, some of the

Hindu customs and traditions have been accepted and carried on as the socio-cultural expressions common to all. Many of the Muslims do not have problem with that. The *namaz* is of course in Arabic, but the *dua* or prayers of petitions are held in Hindi or Urdu. Except for a few vehement clerics, and those elite laity who are associated with fundamentalist groups, generally common Muslims in Varanasi have no difficulty in using terminologies which are specific to Hindu tradition: e.g., *Har har Mahadev* is a common greeting in Varanasi and it is done in the name of Lord Shiva who is the Mahadev and reigning deity and King of Kashi. There are many Muslims in Varanasi city who wish Hindus "*har har mahadev*", and some of them interpret that Allah himself is the Mahadev. It may sound an appeasement of the Hindu community when a Muslim says "*Baba Bholenath ki krupa se....*". But for some it is just repeating "*Insha Allah*" in the language of the common man.

Greeting each other with folded hands is common to Hindus, and Christians have no problem in adapting the same. But there are many Muslims who have accepted this as a norm. Whenever we had poets' meet (*kavya goshthi*) in our centre, organised by a Hindu group, I noticed that the Muslim *shayars*/poets had no difficulty in garlanding the image of goddess Saraswati, (the goddess of knowledge). That symbolic act emerges from the generosity of their hearts.

Culture - Transcendent Muslim Communities

There are Muslim communities in Varanasi and in other parts of Uttar Pradesh who have crossed their religio-cultural borders and inserted themselves into the Hindu culture. Some of these groups are:

Warsi community: The Warsis are followers of Sufi saint Waris Ali Shah of Dewa in Barbanki District or Uttar Pradesh. He was very liberal in his outlook, and travelled a few times to Europe. He asked his Hindu followers to remain in their own religion. There are lakhs of followers of this sect. They address and greet each other as per the Hindu customs. They maintain *mazars*, but the rituals and other customs followed in these *mazars* are similar to Hindu rituals.

Ghosi community: Ghosis of Uttar Pradesh and Bihar claim descent from the Ahir community, and indeed are known as Muslim Ahirs. Traditionally, the Ghosis were a cattle-rearing community, involved in the selling of milk and milk products such as ghee. Ghosi prefer to marry among themselves. They use the surname Khan, which is also used by other pastoral or agricultural Muslim communities of North India. The community is landless, and their main economic activity is the rearing of the cow or buffalo, and selling milk. Many now are employed as labourers as well. They are found throughout North India, and especially in central and eastern Uttar Pradesh. Having a Hindu ancestry, most of the Ghosis live like the Hindus and practice Hindu culture.

The Muslim Nat: Though a large majority of the Nat are Hindus, about 25% of Nat are Muslims. The semi-nomadic Nat Muslims can still be found in acrobatic events and as singers, dancers or unskilled labourers. Tattooing is common for women especially on the forehead. The Nat follow Sunni Muslim traditions and are non-vegetarian. They can be given in child marriages and nuclear families can be more common than extended families among them. The Nat Muslims tend to have a very low literacy rate. Some of them bear Hindu

names. Culturally there is very little difference between them
and Hindus.

Hindus in this Life, Muslims after Death: There is a
community in Varanasi who live as Hindus. But on death, the
dead person is treated as a Muslim. The Maulana comes to say
the last prayers and s/he is buried in the Muslim cemetery. The
post burial ceremonies at home are carried on as per Islamic
tradition. But other living members of the family practice
Hinduism. These people belong to the scavenger caste.

The Conflict of Muslim Women in Interaction with People of Other Faiths

In the male dominant Muslim society, it is the Muslim women
who suffer a lot. There are too many restrictions on them. The
world of the Muslim women is a dark world, unknown to the
outsiders. The Muslim women themselves are kept in dark
and are unaware of the world around. In my observations and
also interactions with Muslim women, I have noticed that the
more they are exposed to the wider society, there is a sort of
awakening which leads to an uprising or revolt to the oppression.
A few of the Muslim women who have broken the restrictions
and come out of their dark world are academics, and elites. But
majority of the Muslim women who have shown the courage to
break the restrictions and male control, are from the financially
weaker sections that had no other options to live, but to break
the taboos imposed on them. Some of them working with us
in our social organisations have abandoned the *hizab/ purdah*.
They have shown the courage to pedal their bicycles to the
working places in spite of taunts, ridicule and threats. In the
process, today they seem to be more empowered than their
counterparts from other religions. It is heartening to see that

those who ridiculed them gradually accept them, give them dignity and even consult them on various issues.

It is obvious that it is poverty that motivates Muslim women to break the shackles of male dominance and social taboos and to get into employment and interaction with people through social organisations. But there are also people with vested interest who have misused the economic deprivation of the Muslim women. In Varanasi, there is a social organisation, backed by the Hindu nationalist organisation, which organises 'dialogue' with Muslim women. Muslim women in *purdah* have been taken to Hindu temples for reciting *Ramcharit Manas* and *Hanuman Chalisa*, to scribble the name of Ram and deposit those papers in the 'Ram Bank' and to do many such things in the name of 'dialogue'. But it has been always a one-sided dialogue. Perhaps they attain a sense of dignity which they do not get in their own community. A teenage girl, who has been with this organisation when she was seven years old, has been given Presidential award during the Republic Day functions in Delhi this year. On the other hand, the network of these marginalized Muslim women living in the economically poor slums has been converted into a political party named 'Muslim Awam Party' which claims that they have 40,000 voters (with 10% male votes). This party founded on the principle of one-sided 'dialogue' campaigned for the ultra-nationalist Hindu party in the 2014 elections. A clear sign of misuse of dialogue for political gains! This is the tip of the iceberg, which floats in the sea of Indian socio-political ocean.

Experience also shows that the genuine dialogue of action with the Muslim women has transformed or rather converted the husbands from being male chauvinists to men of understanding who begin to respect religious diversity, their economic empowerment and gender justice. It proves that genuine dialogue of every sort lights up the dark corners within us, within our homes and society.

Spirituality of Dialogue with Muslims

Dialogue is a call to Perfection. Jesus in his sermon on the mount asked his followers to shun enmity and to break the tradition of the Israel's religious sanction for retributive justice. In Mt 5:43-48, Jesus asks us to "be perfect as the heavenly father is perfect". The perfection of the heavenly father is in his generosity to "make his sun to rise on both the wicked and the good, and he gives rain to the just and the unjust."[5] In the large heart of the heavenly father there is place for all and no place for discrimination on the basis of caste, class, creed and gender. And Jesus wants all his followers to emulate the perfection of the father by going beyond borders, by not limiting the forgiveness and love to one's own community. "Do not even the gentiles do as much?" (Mt.5:47)

Pope Francis said that "God in whom I believe is not a Catholic, but God of all". He has been advocating dialogue in many ways. In his landmark Exhortation Letter encyclical *Evangelii Gaudium*, he calls inter religious dialogue a duty of Christians: "attitude of openness in truth and in love must characterize the dialogue with the followers of non-Christian religions, in spite of various obstacles and difficulties, especially forms of fundamentalism on both sides. Interreligious dialogue is a necessary condition for peace in the world, and so it is a duty for Christians as well as other religious communities."[6] It is a matter of joy that Pope Francis quotes the bishops of India who said that dialogue is a matter of "being open to them, sharing their joys and sorrows".[7] In this way we learn to accept others and their different ways of living, thinking and speaking.

We can then join one another in taking up the duty of serving justice and peace, which should become a basic principle of all our exchanges. A dialogue which seeks social peace and justice is in itself, beyond all merely practical considerations, an ethical commitment which brings about a new social situation.

Salient teachings of Evangelii Gaudium on Dialogue

Beware of Syncretism: Pope Francis warns against the danger of syncretism and relativism in dialogue: "A facile syncretism would ultimately be a totalitarian gesture on the part of those who would ignore greater values of which they are not the masters. True openness involves remaining steadfast in one's deepest convictions, clear and joyful in one's own identity, while at the same time being "open to understanding those of the other party" and "knowing that dialogue can enrich each side".[8] What is not helpful is a diplomatic openness which says 'yes' to everything in order to avoid problems, for this would be a way of deceiving others and denying them the good which we have been given to share generously with others. Evangelization and interreligious dialogue, far from being opposed, mutually support and nourish one another.[9]

Christians and Muslims have a Common Origin: "Our relationship with the followers of Islam has taken on great importance, since they are now significantly present in many traditionally Christian countries, where they can freely worship and become fully a part of society. We must never forget that they "profess to hold the faith of Abraham, and together with us they adore the one, merciful God, who will judge humanity on the last day".[10] The sacred writings of Islam have retained some Christian teachings: Jesus and Mary particularly receive profound veneration.

Muslims Teach us the Discipline of Prayer and Mercy: Muslims both young and old, men and women, make time for daily prayer and faithfully take part in religious services. Many of them also have a deep conviction that their life, in its entirety, is from God and for God. They also acknowledge the need to respond to God with an ethical commitment and with mercy towards those most in need.

Training Required: In order to sustain dialogue with Islam, suitable training is essential for all involved, not only so that they can be solidly and joyfully grounded in their own identity, but so that they can also acknowledge the values of others, appreciate the concerns underlying their demands and shed light on shared beliefs.

Pope Francis Advocates Mutual Hospitality and Freedom: We Christians should embrace with affection and respect Muslim immigrants to our countries in the same way that we hope and ask to be received and respected in countries of Islamic tradition. I ask and I humbly entreat those countries to grant Christians freedom to worship and to practice their faith, in light of the freedom which followers of Islam enjoy in Western countries!

Avoid Generalisations: Faced with disconcerting episodes of violent fundamentalism, our respect for true followers of Islam should lead us to avoid hateful generalisations, for authentic Islam and the proper reading of the Qur'ān are opposed to every form of violence.

Communitarian experience of Journeying towards God: Owing to the sacramental dimension of sanctifying grace, God's working in people of all faiths tends to produce signs and rites, sacred expressions which in turn bring others to a communitarian experience of journeying towards God.[11] As Christians, we can also benefit from these treasures built up over many centuries, which can help us better to live our own beliefs.

Conclusion: Christians' Preparedness for Dialogue with Muslims

To live the spirituality of dialogue which Jesus and the Church propose, we need to train ourselves. A basic disciplining and some precautions are necessary for this. Some requisites for dialogue with Muslims are:

Love for Muslims: If there are prejudices and hateful generalisations, there cannot be a genuine dialogue. Love must be the basic principle and norm. We should approach those with whom we wish to dialogue, with an open heart and give them a place in our hearts.

Be Ready to Stand with and Serve the Muslims in their Struggles: Fr. Norbert Herman, a friend in Udaipur who runs Maitri Sadan, a dialogue centre, *sat* on a *dharna* demanding a passport office for the Haj pilgrims. He won. More than that he won the hearts of the Muslims. They in turn are with him in all his undertakings. As minorities in struggle, we need to support each other.

Respect for Azan: During the call for prayer, broadcast through public sound system, it would be best to stall all activities and remain silent. Resume the activities after seven minutes.

Respect for Holy Qur'ān: Give as much reverence to the Qur'ān as possible. Do not write or print Qur'anic words on paper which can be thrown away. If you find any portion of Qur'ān or even a page, hand it over to a Maulana or any other Muslim person who will either bury it in the ground or allow it to go down into deep waters of a river or well.

Hygienic Purity: Always stay hygienically neat and clean while visiting a religious place of Muslims. If possible perform the ritual wash (*wazu*).

Dealing with Women: We need to be aware that Muslim men expect that while dealing with Muslim women a respectful distance is to be maintained. While talking to a single Muslim woman, they expect that this be done in the company of one more person.

Avoid Enforcing Hindu Customs: Christians should respect the Islamic religious principles and practices. While organising public programs, it is good to avoid typical Hindu ritualistic programs which some Muslims, who are not yet open, may relate to idol worship (e.g: lighting of lamp, garlanding a picture, breaking of coconut etc).

Dialogue is essential for a meaningful human life. Christians have no other option than to dialogue. God brings peace, harmony and fraternity through people who dialogue. When dialogue of reflections, sharing and love leads to dialogue of action for social justice and welfare of all, it transforms the society. When Christians and Muslims, with their own common background, join hands with people of other religions, they will cause miracles in the society. In the process we invite the Muslims also to become 'peacemakers', and thus to be 'sons and daughters of God'. What is required is conviction and a spirituality of love.

Endnotes

[1] J. Dudley Woodberry, *Can We Dialogue with Islam?*, in http://www.christianitytoday.com/ct, Feb 2007, Vol. 51,   No. 2, 108.

[2] Ibid. 109.

[3] Mathew Varghese Anand, *Spirituality of People's Movements for A New Global Order,* A Dissertation Paper for the Degree of Master in Theology, Vidyajyoti, Delhi, 2010, 95.

[4] Asghar Ali Engineer, "Islam-The Ultimate Vision", in *Al- Mushir,* Vol.361/4 (1994), 119

[5] The New Community Bible, St. Paul's, Mumbai, 2008, p. 1658.

[6] Pope Francis, Apostolic Exhortation *Evangelii Gaudium* (Nov. 24, 2013), No.250.

[7] Indian Bishops' Conference, Final Declaration of the XXX Assembly: *The Role of the Church for a Better India* (8 March 2013), 8.9, as quoted in *Evangelii Gaudium,* No. 250

[8] John Paul II, Encyclical Letter *Redemptoris Missio* (7 December 1990), 56: AAS 83 (1991), 304, as quoted in *Evangelii Gaudium,* No. 251.

[9] Cf. Benedict XVI, Address to the Roman Curia (21 December 2012): AAS 105 (2006), 51; Second Vatican Ecumenical Council, Decree on the Missionary Activity of the Church *Ad Gentes*, 9; *Catechism of the Catholic Church*, 856, as quoted in *Evangelii Gaudium,* No. 251

[10] Second Vatican Ecumenical Council, Dogmatic Constitution on the Church *Lumen Gentium*, 16, as quoted in *Evangelii Gaudium,* No. 252

[11] International Theological Commission, *Christianity and the World Religions* (1996), 72: *Enchiridion Vaticanum* 15, Nos. 1070-1076, as quoted in *Evangelii Gaudium,* No. 254.

Religious Cosmopolitanism as the Key to Peace and Harmony in the Third Millennium

Jerome Sylvester IMS

Religious experience is quite complex in the context of plurality of religions and cultures. It could be illustrated with an example from India. Most citizens in India wake up to the *suprabhadam* (morning songs) of the temple with the intermittent call for *hazan* (invitation for prayer) from the nearby Mosques and the pealing of bells for the *angelus* from a Church, followed by a reading from the Bible. It is a unique experience of religious plurality which unconsciously drilled into the minds of the people living in that locality. During festivals of the communities children would be asked to carry sweetmeats (variety of sweet edibles) prepared for the feast according to the religio-cultural ethos. On such occasions, exchange of greeting and best wishes from members of other communities are quite normal and are expected to be reciprocated with sense of harmony as a natural outflow of fellowship and peace. These experiences are translated into philosophies of life such as *'jiyo jine do'* (live let live). Thus, 'Unity in diversity' became part of the philosophy of life of a nation with plurality of cultures, languages and religions.

In short, and as a reflection, the paradigmatic way one lives together as Hindus, Christians and Muslims is the daily experience of vast majority of Indians. Communities depend on each other in economic and social spheres. Muslims buy agricultural products from Christians and Hindus and are very much part of the community. But, on the one hand, there is a sense of mutual relationship and cordiality and, on the other, there are also religious prejudices, and exclusivism exists in covert forms. But such differences were never discussed or came in the way of otherwise good relationship thanks to post-Vatican sense of Christian openness towards other faiths and religions. The reality of pluralistic living is same in the cities all over India, but in the rural areas, people are isolated as communities in villages; such as *gaou* (Village), *basti*, *tolla*s (settlements of huts) *pahi* (simple living by the fields with the farm animals), etc...[1] This situation of isolation and demarcation influences one's thinking and being in the pluralist society.

Unity in Plurality is etched in the very fabric of Indian culture and history. Poets and philosophers of India extolled diversity as a unique gift of the country. The great poet of undivided India, Iqbal, in his soulful song, *"Sare jahan se Acha"*[2] compared Indian society to a 'guldasta' i.e. a bouquet of different flowers.[3] The national anthem epitomizes the great cultural and linguistic diversity of India. The national flag is a symbol of the religious and geographical diversity of the country. But this unity of India in its diversity has been threatened time and again in the course of history by inter-religious conflicts and communal violence. Yet, the resolve of the vast majority of Indian people to protect the plurality and the unity that underlies it remain undiminished.[4]

From the above narratives of experience from the context and from what I have heard from others I would like to reflect on the Christian Theology of Religions from three strands: 1) The tradition of pluralism within the Hindu tradition. The various sects such as *Saivism, Vaishnavism, Tantrisims, Sakthas,* and Native Religions; 2) Inter-religious pluralism in relation to the major religions in India - Indian-Christian[5] encounters and experiences of spiritual and social well-being and 3) The present context of inter-religious dialogue and living in India with the socio-political interaction.

The development of various sects in Hinduism could be very well traced in history. Apart from the *Smriti* and *Sruti* classical tradition, the proto-type such as Indra with later Siva and the culmination of Saivism with *Sivajnana podagam, Thiruvasagam,* as classical texts, and many of myths *puranas* related to Siva-Ganga to Siva Linga worship are inheritance of the Indian Masses. It is a religion of monotheism and social equality of humans. Saivism considers Siva as the *Purusha* (the primordial being) and *prakrithi* (the created). Knowledge and devotion are the way to attain the destiny. Vaishnavism has developed as religious sect as the history of Avatars proliferated. It gave rise to *Kathas, Mahatmiyams* of different *trithas* and epics like *Mahabharat* and *Ramayan.* Later, the Viashnava texts were interpreted and developed into Vadakalai and Thennkalai. Today, popular cults like *Ram Lila, Krishna Katha*[6] are evidence to their vibrancy. It is polytheistic religion and emphasis is more on the side of ritual actions, belief in rebirth (*karma and punarjanma*). Concepts of social stratification, purity and profane are prevalent among them. One has to be born a Brahmin to attain liberation (*mukti*).

Though one does not know exactly the origins of the worship of mother Goddess, from the time of Indus civilisation, it has not been obliterated by any religious upheavals. It is the most popular form of worship and spread in all part of the country. If only humanity could ever unravel the mystery of origin of human life, then we may also know the origins of fertility cults. In the same sense, both practise of different types of *tantr- mantr* and sensibilities of Native religions could be discovered as part of the religious heritage and culture of plurality.

The doctrines of each sect of Hinduism are so variant and diverse. Dialogue would be a process of coming to know the other from point of difference and convergence. To know the other partner in dialogue is the first step to relationship.

Islam, from its early days, has been known for its two sects as Shia and Sunni. In India, Islam has its off shot known as Sufism. It is rightly said that Islam was adapted to the culture of the land and it has elements of Bhakti traditions of India. Devout Muslims are both patriotic and religious. Their love for peace and harmony is also evident in many National issues.

Christianity in India has the same longevity of its history as either of Ephesus or Rome or Alexandria. It came with St. Thomas, one of the Apostles of Jesus Christ and subsequent visitors, traders and settlers. Christianity has been here ever since the first century AD embedded within the cultural ethos of the nation. It was time and again confronted and misunderstood by the visitors and colonists during the last five hundred years. Its contribution to the nation for the last two millennia is a historiography to be recovered.

The Present Scenario

There are few points to be considered. The first one emerges from the present scenario of plurality of culture, language and religion which are under pressure and challenged by forces of narrow interpretation of nationalism and projection of particular language or culture on all. This is a regression and assault on culture of *unity in diversity*, the soul of the Indian Nation.

The second emerges from the church's practise of dialogue in Asia. The FABC directed the dialogue in Asia to be as triple dialogue: with religions, with poor and cultures/ideologies. There are many centres for dialogue with religion and cultures with organised programmes for mutual understanding. But the significant dialogue was with the poor and marginalised. The dialogue with the poor has not only resulted in projects for socio-educational developments but networking of like-minded people. It leads people of different communities and religions to think to gather and respond to social issues. It has also brought people of good will to address social cause and at times of needs like communal riots and natural disasters.

The third point to be considered is called dialogue of life. In the process of life many people have chosen to live with people of other religions for collaboration for social cause, such as development, models of peace and harmonious living is a divided society. Some have taken to live as families of Interfaith. We should recognise the sense of responsibility and risk taken by these volunteers of dialogue. Their sense of respect for other's faith and culture is also gift of new understanding and efforts in dialogue.

The above resume and analysis leads us to differentiate our stand from the earlier positions. I may call it, provisionally, the pluralist deference, respect for the plurality of culture, language and religions thriving in India.

Pluralist Deference

In the Post Vatican II scenario, while the West was discussing in the line of inclusivism[7] and grappling with the sudden outburst of diversity in Europe and Americas as the consequence of globalisation, theology of religions becomes a cumbersome compulsion for co-existence. It also prompts to reflect on in line with universal and responsible living in the society. Paul Knitter has come out with his idea of calling himself a *mutualist* rather than pluralist or even the idea of *double belonging* of Michael Amaladoss. They are trying to venture beyond Pluralism and Exclusivism.

There are two aspects to the living experience in the context of Asia, especially in India.

1. The situation neither allows an exclusion or inclusion, because of the subtlety of *Varna* System of social stratification. The mode of present existence could be seen as *non-exclusivism.* Neither it excludes nor does it include all. It is part-and-apart. This pluralist deference necessarily enters the second level. The second level of necessity emerges from the need to political consensus for the development and progress of the human society; call it, to the eschatological fulfilment. The socio-political situation of globalization and resource mobilization leads to a change in the understanding of co-existence. If entire humanity is one family the new forms of socio-economic exclusion, systemic exploitation have to be addressed. There is a moral imperative behind it. It needs political will, which is discussed often under the concept of cosmopolitanism.

2. The moral imperative directly links with the normative role
    of religion in the society. Therefore, the discussion on, both,
    religion and cosmopolitanism becomes the key Theology
    of Religions, a source for peace and harmony.

Cosmopolitanism

Cosmopolitanism is a demanding and contentious moral position.
It urges us to embrace the whole world into our moral concerns
and to apply the standards of impartiality and equity across
boundaries of nationality, race, and gender in a way that would
have been unheard of even fifty years ago. It suggests a range
of virtues which the cosmopolitan individual should display
virtues such as tolerance, justice, pity, righteous indignation at
injustice, generosity toward the poor and starving, care for the
global environment, and the willingness to take responsibility
for change on a global scale. Cosmopolitanism has relevance
for international distributive justice; peace; human rights;
environmental sustainability; protection for minorities, refugees
and other oppressed groups; democratic participation; and inter-
cultural tolerance. Cosmopolitanism addresses the ethical issues
inherent in modern societies and identifies the moral obligations
that individuals, multinational corporations and governments
might have in relation to them. While espousing a cosmopolitan
form of global ethics, a liberal form of politics, sustainable and
just forms of business practice, and an internationalist approach
to global conflict and governance, it seeks to present as many
sides of the ethical debates as can be supported by reasonable
argument. One may discuss the work of Kwame Anthony
Appiah, Seyla Benhabib, Martha Nussbaum, Thomas Pogge,
John Rawls, Amartya Sen, Henry Shue, Peter Singer and others,
this line to understand cosmopolitanism and analyses the reality
of the rights and responsibilities that it espouses.

Religious Experience and Enculturation

In the recent decades, the marginalised and downtrodden in the Indian society have found recourse to religion for their socio-spiritual empowerment. For instance, the spirituality of *Khristubhaktas* emerges from the grassroots, from the spirituality of their own, influenced by Hindu Bhakti movement. Bhakti movement in itself enshrines openness to *Ishtadevata* – the deity who responds to one's spiritual inclinations and quest. The Bhakti movement allows the choice for the devotees to commit themselves passionately to an *Ishtadevata.* The new search for identity of *Khristbhaktas* finds a response in the teachings of Jesus and in the experience of his person, and he becomes their *Ishtadevata* – personal deity. The message of this *Ishtadevata* - Jesus - appropriated and interpreted by them becomes a liberating experience. We see how crucial the subjectivity of the believer and his or her appropriation is, unlike in an approach of communication of faith.[8]

Here we are in the face of an appropriation of Christian faith in a unique way and selectively determined by the concrete circumstances and history of a people, rather than an abstract communication of faith divorced from the concrete history of the subjects involved. The axis shifts to the agency of those who begin to experience Christian faith and build a new identity with a new worldview of emancipation and dignity deploring all forms of victimhood and exclusion. This immediacy of the subaltern people and their quest for socio-economic empowerment, liberation from various forms of oppressions and final salvation impels them to a new way of understanding their situation cleansed by the light of the Gospel. This new socio-political-religious consciousness is essential for the humanity today.

In the context of bhakti, the idea of holiness as 'perfection', which in practice is identified with orderliness and uniformity, the *Khristbhaktas* express themselves in simplicity and in a wide variety of ways that cannot be classified. Moreover, the faith experience of *Khristbhaktas* does not involve any change in their traditional cultural expressions and rites. For example, they continue with the traditional wedding rituals. Their being *Khristbhaktas* does not bring about any change in their cultural practices. Moreover, the *Khristbhaktas* in some areas bring their infants to the centres of common worship and get their children named. It could be viewed as an initiation into faith-experience, and not as baptism. The osmosis of cultural worlds is not just adaptation or inculturation. It is real mutual fecundation of cultures resulting in enculturation.

Communion of communities as Authority

It is important to note that the community of *Khristbhaktas* does not have a fixed place for gathering or for worship and structures. Wherever people gather in faith, there 'the community happens'. The place of worship for them is not something separate and exclusive. This means that different other activities could take place in the same place as the worship. It also means that *Khristbhaktas* have a strong sense of mobility, in as much as the concept of sacred place is not fixed, but relative to the actual coming together of the members of the community. When faith communities link with each other and exercise their social role, they realise the core of cosmopolitanism in potency.

Khristbhakta Movement: An emerging model of Religious Cosmopolitanism

What is happening in the *Khristbhakta* movement is 'faith encountering faith' in the deeper subjecthood of the believer.

The dialogue the *Khristbhaktas* enter into with the Christian experience is shaped already by their experience of faith in Hinduism and other indigenous religious traditions. The encounter with the Christian experience deepens their experience nurtured through their traditional rites, practices, etc. The oft-repeated allegation of syncretism or double-loyalty in such cases stand challenged. There is on the one hand an appropriation of Christian faith through the experience of faith already nurtured by their religious tradition. And at the same time, their faith reaches organically another level of depth in the encounter with Christianity. The case of *Khristbhaktas* is one of faith-journey, one to another not as discontinuity, but as snow balling into transformation. There is no break with one's past religious experience to embrace a totally new faith and message. The experience and spiritual process the *Khristbhaktas* undergo is a journey in which their past accompanies them while they move ahead in their faith-quest. We have in their experience the meeting of two worlds of religious experience. In short, the experience of *Khristbhaktas* could be characterized as religious cosmopolitanism.

The simple fact is that religions belong to the entire humanity. "By religious cosmopolitanism is meant the basic attitude and the attendant mode of practice that considers that all religions are the heritage of humanity. It is a mode of existence in which a person has the ability to enter into the religious world of the other. It is a deeply human and spiritual attitude. If political cosmopolitanism is rooted in one's particular nation, but at the same time open to others, so is also the case of religious cosmopolitanism. What religious cosmopolitanism does is to challenge religious ontology identified with doctrines, laws, and regulations just like political cosmopolitanism challenges national ontology. Therefore, religious cosmopolitanism tends to bridge religions as a communion of communities."⁹

The communion of communities would be a challenge for those who think of absolutism and monopoly of truth and to those forces that play a destructive role when they begin to compare each other or want to demonstrate the superiority of one over the other. Religious cosmopolitanism enshrines within self a critique of historicity of religions. The openness of the faith-community to see itself as part of the universal human community is the global consciousness of unity of destiny. This spirit of religious cosmopolitanism implies that by fostering the world community that one fosters one's own faith-community and allows other with a spirit of non-exclusivism. As St Paul says, "if one member suffers all suffer together with it; if one member is honoured all rejoice together with it" (Cf. 1 Cor 12:26). As all religions belong to humanity, if one faith-community suffers the whole humanity suffers. If one community inflicts pain still the whole humanity suffers. It is good to protect and honour the whole than only parts.

A socially responsible citizen with enduring religious value is sure to think of the well-being of another. In other words, only those who get convinced of religious cosmopolitanism could work for lasting peace and harmony in a pluralist society. The spirituality of dialogue could be the sense of being responsible and active member of the human community with a sense of respect and responsibility for others. This sense of cosmopolitan presence of religions in Religious Cosmopolitanism is envisaged as Spirituality of Dialogue.

Endnotes

[1] Sociologist and ethnographers describe them as another form of social stratification, another form of social exclusion.

[2] '*Sare Jahan Se Acha*' when translated, means 'India, the most beautiful country in the world'. One of the main reasons that the poet cites for the beauty of the country is its religious and cultural diversity. This song is almost next to the national anthem in its popularity and is often sung in common gatherings. Interview: Thomas Chillikulam, SJ, Varanasi, 2009.

[3] Paul Knitter, *Religious Pluralism and Religious Imagination* (Conference Paper) KU Leuven, 2000.

[4] Interview: Thomas Chillikulam SJ, Varanasi, 2009.

[5] A study of the demography and ethnography of Christian communities in India reveals its diversity. The difference are evident when compared as communities at different river banks civilizations such as Indus Valley, Gangatic plains, Chambal and Narmada *ghats,* Godavari and Krishna plateau, Vaikai and Kaveri belt. The cultures and languages of each area differ significantly as moves from one to the other. This diversity is never compromised for the sake of unity. Uniformity was never thought of as a form of unity in this land. It was the political will of Great Emperors and Vassals that kept the unity. Kings were ready to negotiate monogamy or polygamy for political consolidations as a county and Nation.

[6] A study based on Oral Formulaic Theory and Performance Theory from Folklorists highlights many of these dimensions. Cf. Jerome Sylvester, *Hermeneutics of Story Telling,* (M. Phil dissertation. University of Madras, Chennai, 2003).

[7] Anonymous Christians – a concept developed by Karl Rahner and Unknown Christ of Hinduism and so on.

[8] In this context, I may adduce here the example of a woman *Khristbhakta* from Varanasi of 35 years of age. She was attending the *satsang.* In her eagerness to know more about Christianity, she had bought a Bible, even though she did not know how to read, unlettered as she was. But when she listened to the parable of the ten virgins being read out, she identified herself as a foolish virgin, since she had the Bible and yet could not read. This led her to learn the alphabets to read by herself the Bible. Now she has become the local interpreter of the Christian message to other women and *Khristbhaktas.* This is a clear proof of the unique value of appropriation of faith, which in no way can be substituted by communication of faith.

[9] Felix Wilfred, *Margins*, (Delhi: ISPCK, 2008), 162.

Appendix - I

Second Vatican Council
Declaration on
the Relation of the Church to Non-christian Religions
Nostra Aetate
proclaimed by his holiness
Pope Paul VI
on October 28, 1965

1. In our time, when day by day mankind is being drawn closer together, and the ties between different peoples are becoming stronger, the Church examines more closely her relationship to non-Christian religions. In her task of promoting unity and love among men, indeed among nations, she considers above all in this declaration what men have in common and what draws them to fellowship.

One is the community of all peoples, one their origin, for God made the whole human race to live over the face of the earth.[1] One also is their final goal, God. His providence, His manifestations of goodness, His saving design extend to all men,[2] until that time when the elect will be united in the Holy City, the city ablaze with the glory of God, where the nations

will walk in His light.[3] Men expect from the various religions
answers to the unsolved riddles of the human condition, which
today, even as in former times, deeply stir the hearts of men:
What is man? What is the meaning, the aim of our life? What
is moral good, what is sin? Whence suffering and what purpose
does it serve? Which is the road to true happiness? What are
death, judgment and retribution after death? What, finally, is
that ultimate inexpressible mystery which encompasses our
existence: whence do we come, and where are we going?

2. From ancient times down to the present, there is found
    among various peoples a certain perception of that hidden
    power which hovers over the course of things and over the
    events of human history; at times some indeed have come
    to the recognition of a Supreme Being, or even of a Father.
    This perception and recognition penetrates their lives with
    a profound religious sense.

Religions, however, that are bound up with an advanced culture
have struggled to answer the same questions by means of more
refined concepts and a more developed language. Thus, in
Hinduism, men contemplate the divine mystery and express
it through an inexhaustible abundance of myths and through
searching philosophical inquiry. They seek freedom from
the anguish of our human condition either through ascetical
practices or profound meditation or a flight to God with love
and trust. Again, Buddhism, in its various forms, realizes the
radical insufficiency of this changeable world; it teaches a way
by which men, in a devout and confident spirit, may be able
either to acquire the state of perfect liberation, or attain, by
their own efforts or through higher help, supreme illumination.
Likewise, other religions found everywhere try to counter the
restlessness of the human heart, each in its own manner, by

proposing "ways," comprising teachings, rules of life, and sacred rites. The Catholic Church rejects nothing that is true and holy in these religions. She regards with sincere reverence those ways of conduct and of life, those precepts and teachings which, though differing in many aspects from the ones she holds and sets forth, nonetheless often reflect a ray of that Truth which enlightens all men. Indeed, she proclaims, and ever must proclaim Christ "the way, the truth, and the life" (John 14:6), in whom men may find the fullness of religious life, in whom God has reconciled all things to Himself.[4] The Church, therefore, exhorts her sons, that through dialogue and collaboration with the followers of other religions, carried out with prudence and love and in witness to the Christian faith and life, they recognize, preserve and promote the good things, spiritual and moral, as well as the socio-cultural values found among these men.

3. The Church regards with esteem also the Moslems. They adore the one God, living and subsisting in Himself; merciful and all- powerful, the Creator of heaven and earth,[5] who has spoken to men; they take pains to submit wholeheartedly to even His inscrutable decrees, just as Abraham, with whom the faith of Islam takes pleasure in linking itself, submitted to God. Though they do not acknowledge Jesus as God, they revere Him as a prophet. They also honor Mary, His virgin Mother; at times they even call on her with devotion. In addition, they await the day of judgment when God will render their deserts to all those who have been raised up from the dead. Finally, they value the moral life and worship God especially through prayer, almsgiving and fasting.

Since in the course of centuries not a few quarrels and hostilities have arisen between Christians and Muslims, this sacred synod urges all to forget the past and to work sincerely for mutual understanding and to preserve as well as to promote together for the benefit of all mankind social justice and moral welfare, as well as peace and freedom.

4. As the sacred synod searches into the mystery of the Church, it remembers the bond that spiritually ties the people of the New Covenant to Abraham's stock.

Thus, the Church of Christ acknowledges that, according to God's saving design, the beginnings of her faith and her election are found already among the Patriarchs, Moses and the prophets. She professes that all who believe in Christ-Abraham's sons according to faith[6] are included in the same Patriarch's call, and likewise that the salvation of the Church is mysteriously foreshadowed by the chosen people's exodus from the land of bondage. The Church, therefore, cannot forget that she received the revelation of the Old Testament through the people with whom God in His inexpressible mercy concluded the Ancient Covenant. Nor can she forget that she draws sustenance from the root of that well-cultivated olive tree onto which have been grafted the wild shoots, the Gentiles.[7] Indeed, the Church believes that by His cross Christ, Our Peace, reconciled Jews and Gentiles. making both one in Himself.[8] The Church keeps ever in mind the words of the Apostle about his kinsmen: "theirs is the sonship and the glory and the covenants and the law and the worship and the promises; theirs are the fathers and from them is the Christ according to the flesh" (Rom. 9:4-5), the Son of the Virgin Mary. She also recalls that the Apostles, the Church's main-stay and pillars, as well as most of the early disciples who proclaimed Christ's Gospel to the world, sprang from the Jewish people.

As Holy Scripture testifies, Jerusalem did not recognize the time of her visitation,[9] nor did the Jews in large number, accept the Gospel; indeed not a few opposed its spreading.[10] Nevertheless, God holds the Jews most dear for the sake of their Fathers; He does not repent of the gifts He makes or of the calls He issues-such is the witness of the Apostle.[11] In company with the Prophets and the same Apostle, the Church awaits that day, known to God alone, on which all peoples will address the Lord in a single voice and "serve him shoulder to shoulder" (Soph. 3:9).[12]

Since the spiritual patrimony common to Christians and Jews is thus so great, this sacred synod wants to foster and recommend that mutual understanding and respect which is the fruit, above all, of biblical and theological studies as well as of fraternal dialogues.

True, the Jewish authorities and those who followed their lead pressed for the death of Christ;[13] still, what happened in His passion cannot be charged against all the Jews, without distinction, then alive, nor against the Jews of today. Although the Church is the new people of God, the Jews should not be presented as rejected or accursed by God, as if this followed from the Holy Scriptures. All should see to it, then, that in catechetical work or in the preaching of the word of God they do not teach anything that does not conform to the truth of the Gospel and the spirit of Christ.

Furthermore, in her rejection of every persecution against any man, the Church, mindful of the patrimony she shares with the Jews and moved not by political reasons but by the Gospel's spiritual love, decries hatred, persecutions, displays of anti-Semitism, directed against Jews at any time and by anyone.

Besides, as the Church has always held and holds now, Christ underwent His passion and death freely, because of the sins of men and out of infinite love, in order that all may reach salvation. It is, therefore, the burden of the Church's preaching to proclaim the cross of Christ as the sign of God's all-embracing love and as the fountain from which every grace flows.

5. We cannot truly call on God, the Father of all, if we refuse to treat in a brotherly way any man, created as he is in the image of God. Man's relation to God the Father and his relation to men his brothers are so linked together that Scripture says: "He who does not love does not know God" (1 John 4:8).

No foundation therefore remains for any theory or practice that leads to discrimination between man and man or people and people, so far as their human dignity and the rights flowing from it are concerned.

The Church reproves, as foreign to the mind of Christ, any discrimination against men or harassment of them because of their race, color, condition of life, or religion. On the contrary, following in the footsteps of the holy Apostles Peter and Paul, this sacred synod ardently implores the Christian faithful to "maintain good fellowship among the nations" (1 Peter 2:12), and, if possible, to live for their part in peace with all men,[14] so that they may truly be sons of the Father who is in heaven.[15]

Endnotes

[1] Cf. *Acts* 17:26.

[2] Cf. *Wis.* 8:1; *Acts* 14:17; *Rom.* 2:6-7; 1 *Tim.* 2:4.

[3] Cf. *Apoc.* 21:23f.

[4] Cf 2 *Cor.* 5:18-19

[5] Cf St. Gregory VII, *letter XXI to Anzir (Nacir), King of Mauritania* (Pl. 148, col. 450f.)

[6] Cf. *Gal.* 3:7

[7] Cf. *Rom.* 11:17-24

[8] Cf. *Eph.* 2:14-16

9 Cf. *Lk.* 19:44

[10] Cf. *Rom.* 11:28

[11] Cf. *Rom.* 11:28-29; cf. dogmatic Constitution, *Lumen Gentium* (Light of nations) AAS, 57 (1965) pag. 20

[12] Cf. *Is.* 66:23; *Ps.* 65:4; *Rom.* 11:11-32

[13] Cf. *John.* 19:6

[14] Cf. *Rom.* 12:18

[15] Cf. *Matt.* 5:45

Appendix - II

Pontifical Council for Interreligious Dialogue

Letter to Presidents of Bishops' Conferences on the Spirituality of Dialogue[1]

Your Excellency,

1. Though there have always been contacts between Catholics and the followers of other religions, the Second Vatican Council, and in particular the Declaration Nostra Aetate, can be considered a watershed in these relations. It brought about a renewal in the outlook of the Church towards other religions. In the intervening years, guided by the teaching of the Pontifical Magisterium and by such documents as The Attitude of the Church toward the Followers of Other Religions (1984) and Dialogue and Proclamation (1991), Catholics have been making considerable efforts to meet the followers of other religions. They have undertaken various initiatives and, with time, these have increased in number and become more widespread. Encounters with people of other religions occur at the level of daily life, in the joint

promotion of social projects, in the exchange of religious experience, and in formal exchanges where Christians and other believers discuss elements of belief or practice. Catholics and other Christians engaged in such interreligious dialogue are becoming more and more convinced of the need of a sound Christian spirituality to uphold their efforts. The Christian who meets other believers is not involved in an activity which is marginal to his or her faith. Rather is it something which arises from the demands of that faith. It flows from faith and should be nourished by faith. In October 1998 the Pontifical Council for Interreligious Dialogue took the Spirituality of Dialogue as the theme of its Plenary Assembly. At the end of the Assembly the Members thought it would be useful to share some of the reflections with our brothers in the episcopate around the world. They asked me to write to you to report on some of the considerations put forward during our meeting, and to request your reaction in view of an eventual document from our Council.

2. God is love and communion

    God is love and communion. As St John tells us, God is love (cf 1 Jn 4:16). The mystery of the Most Blessed Trinity reveals to us that the Eternal Father loves the Son, the Son loves the Father, and this mutual love of the Father and the Son is the Person of the Holy Spirit. Moreover, the Father communicates himself entirely to the Son who is God from God, Light from Light. The Holy Spirit who proceeds from the Father and the Son is together with the Father and the Son one God who is communion in the depth of his mystery. This Trinitarian mystery of love and communion is the eminent model for human relations and the foundation of dialogue.

3. God communicates himself to humankind

    Out of his bountiful love God decided to communicate himself to the human beings that he had created. The Only-Begotten Son of God took on human nature in order "to gather the scattered children of God" (Jn 11:52), to restore communion between humanity and God, to communicate divine life to people and finally to bring them to the eternal vision of God. The Incarnation is the supreme manifestation of God's saving will. It is the way chosen by God to go in search of the human being, damaged and estranged from God by original sin, as the shepherd goes in search of the lost sheep. Incarnation means, on the one hand, that the Son of God assumed all that is positive in human nature. On the other hand, it takes the form of kenosis. As St Paul writes to the Philippians: "Have this mind among yourselves, which was in Christ Jesus, who, though he was in the form of God, did not count equality with God a thing to be grasped, but emptied himself, taking the form of a servant, being born in the likeness of men. And being found in human form he humbled himself and became obedient unto death, even death on a cross" (Phil 2:5-8). This was the way chosen in the divine plan to re-establish communion between humankind and God, to recapitulate all things so that finally "God may be all in all" (1 Cor 15:28; cf. Eph 1:15). So, when Christians meet other believers, they are called to have the mind of Christ, to follow in his footsteps.

4. Conversion to God

    The Christian who wishes to enter into contact and establish collaboration with other believers must strive first of all to be converted to God. In this context conversion to God is understood as openness to the action of the Holy Spirit within oneself, seeking positively to discern the will of God, and readiness to do this will when it is known. The Christian is aware that everyone is bound to search for the will of God and to obey it as it is made known by informed conscience. Everyone can, and should, make progress in this commitment to seek and do God's will. Moreover, the more the partners in interreligious dialogue "seek the face of God" (cf. Ps 27:8), the nearer they will come to each other and the better chance they will have of understanding each other. It can be seen, therefore, that interreligious dialogue is a deeply religious activity.

5. Christian identity in dialogue
    The Christian who meets other believers does so as a member of the Christian faith community, and therefore as a witness to Jesus Christ. It is important that the Christian should have a clear religious identity. Interreligious dialogue does not demand that the Christian should set some elements of Christian belief or practice aside, putting them as it were between parentheses, much less putting them in doubt. On the contrary, other believers want to know clearly whom they are meeting.

It is our firm conviction that God wants all persons to be saved (cf 1 Tim 2:4) and that God can give his grace also outside the visible boundaries of the Church (cf LG 16; Redemptor Hominis 10). At the same time the Christian is aware that Jesus Christ, the Son of God made man, is the one and only Saviour of all humanity, and that only in the Church which Christ founded are to be found the means of salvation in all their fulness. This should in no way induce the Christian to assume a triumphalistic attitude or to act out of a superiority complex. On the contrary, it is with humility and with a desire for mutual enrichment that one will meet with other believers, while holding firmly to the truths of the Christian faith. Interreligious dialogue, when conducted in this vision of faith, in no way leads to religious relativism.

6. Proclamation and dialogue

In dialogue the Christian is called to be a witness to Christ, imitating the Lord in his proclamation of the Kingdom, his concern and compassion for each individual person and his respect for that person's liberty. There is a need to rediscover the close connection between proclamation and dialogue as elements of the evangelizing mission of the Church (cf Dialogue and Proclamation 77-85). It will be seen that these elements are not interchangeable, nor are they to be confused, yet they are indeed related (cf Redemptoris Missio 55). Proclamation aims at conversion in the sense of free acceptance of the Good News of Christ and becoming a member of the Church. Dialogue, on the other hand, presupposes conversion in the sense of a return of the heart to God in love and obedience to His will, in other words, openness of the heart to the action of God (cf. The Attitude of the Church toward the Followers of other Religions 37). It is God who attracts people to himself, sending his Spirit who is at work in the depths of their hearts.

7. The need to understand other believers

The Christian who engages in interreligious initiatives feels more and more the need to understand other religions in order precisely to understand better the followers of these religions. It will be seen that there are many points of contact: belief in one God who is Creator, the aspiration to transcendence, the practice of fasting and almsgiving, recourse to prayer and meditation, the importance of pilgrimage. The differences, however, should not be overlooked. A Christian spirituality of dialogue will grow if both these dimensions are maintained. While appreciating the workings of the Spirit of God among people of other religions, not only in the hearts of individuals but also in some of their religious rites (cf RM 55), the uniqueness of the Christian faith will be respected.

8. In faith, hope and charity the spirituality which is to animate and uphold interreligious dialogue is one which is lived out in faith, hope and charity. There is faith in God, who is the Creator and Father of the whole of humanity, who dwells in light inaccessible and whose mystery the human mind is incapable of penetrating. Hope characterises a dialogue which does not demand to see instant results, but holds on firmly to the belief that "dialogue is a path towards the Kingdom and will certainly bear fruit, even if the time and seasons are known only to the Father (cf Acts 1:7)" (RM 57). Charity which comes from God, and is communicated to us by the Holy Spirit, urges the Christian to share God's love with other believers in a gratuitous way. The Christian is therefore convinced that interreligious activity flows out of the heart of the Christian faith.

9. Nourished by prayer and sacrifice. This spirituality is nourished by prayer and sacrifice. Prayer links the Christian with the goodness and power of God without whom we can do nothing (cf Jn 15:5). Without God's life-giving action, mere human activity is not able to affect any permanent spiritual good. Sacrifice strengthens prayer and promotes

communion with others. Christians learn from their faith to love other believers even when the latter apparently do not reciprocate, or at least not immediately. The teaching of Christ is that we must love with detachment, that we should be ready to walk the extra mile, that we should not look for revenge if we suffer wrong doing but rather seek to overcome evil by good. This is a sign not of weakness, but of spiritual strength.

10. Your suggestions in communicating the above reflections of our Plenary Assembly to our brothers in the episcopate, through you, the Presidents of the Bishops' Conferences, I wish to ask for your own reflections and suggestions. It is obvious that these will take into account the experience of interreligious dialogue in your area, the difficulties encountered but also the fruits that have been evident. I would be grateful if your answer could reach me before September 1999. It will be extremely helpful to our Pontifical Council in the preparation of an eventual document on the Spirituality of Dialogue. Thanking you for your kind cooperation, I remain, Devotedly Yours in Christ Francis Cardinal Arinze President Vatican City: 3 March, 1999

Towards a document on the Spirituality of Dialogue.

Endnotes

[1] http://groups.creighton.edu/sjdialogue/documents/articles/spirituality_of_ dialogue.html   (last visit on Feb. 20, 2019); italian version: http://www. internetica.it/dialogo_spiritualita.htm (last visit March 28, 2019).

Appendix - III

Address of his Holiness John Paul II to Participants in the Plenary Assembly of the Pontifical Council for Interreligious Dialogue

Hall of Popes, Friday, 24 November 1995

Dear Cardinal Arinze,

Your Eminences,

Dear Brother Bishops, and Friends in Christ,

1. I am happy to have this occasion to meet the members of the Pontifical Council for Interreligious Dialogue gathered for your Plenary Assembly. I greet you in the peace of Christ, through whom "we have obtained access to this grace in which we stand, and we rejoice in our hope of sharing the glory of God" (Rom. 5:2).

   Thirty years after the Council issued the Declaration on the relationship of the Church to non-Christian Religions, your involvement in interreligious dialogue cannot but continue to be guided and encouraged by the teaching and insights of that important document. Indeed, the theme of your Assembly, 'The Dialogue of Spirituality and the Spirituality of Dialogue', provides an excellent opportunity for reflection on what might be called "the reading of the human soul", which is the starting point of "Nostra Aetate", which states: "Men look to their different religions for an answer to the unsolved riddles of human existence... What is man? What is the meaning and purpose of life? What is upright behaviour, and what is sinful? Where does suffering originate, and what end does it serve? How can genuine happiness be found? What happens at death? What is judgment? What reward follows death? And finally, what is the ultimate mystery, beyond human explanation, which embraces our entire existence, from which we take our origin and towards which we tend?" (Nostra Aetate, 1).

2. Often today, in many parts of the world, a materialistic culture imprisons people as it were in space and time, so that they find themselves disorientated and unable to give meaning to life. Some, as the Second Vatican Council already noted, living in an atmosphere of practical materialism, do not perceive this human drama (cf. Gaudium et Spes, 10). There are others "whose hopes are set on a genuine and total emancipation of mankind through human effort alone and look forward to some future earthly paradise where all the desires of their hearts will be fulfilled" (Ibid.). A third category, those who believe in God or search for the Absolute, finds a response to these interrogations of the human soul through spirituality, in other words through a conception of life and of human history which is not

confined to the narrow limits of our earthly existence, but which is open to transcendence and to eternity. The Church, for her part, "believes that Christ, who died and was raised for the sake of all, can show man the way and strengthen him through the Spirit in order to be worthy of his destiny". She believes too that "the key, the centre and the purpose of the whole of man's history are to be found in the Lord and Master" (Ibid.).

3. The "spirituality" which is at the heart of your reflections involves the concept of man's quest for a personal relationship with God, a relationship which can give life and substance to his relations with others who follow a different religious tradition. "Spirituality" is more than knowledge and discussion. It is inseparable from the search for holiness which, in the absolute sense, belongs only to God, but which, through his tender mercy, is given also to man as a gift and a responsibility. The Second Vatican Council has re-echoed the exhortation of St Paul: "What God wants is for you all to be holy" (1 Thess. 4:3), underlining on more than one occasion the universal vocation to holiness ((cf. Lumen Gentium, 42).

In the wider perspective, the search for perfection, for purification, for conformity to the divine will is not restricted to Christians. It involves every human being. It is no wonder therefore that we find in the religious traditions of humanity a clear awareness of the call to the highest values. The various religions, as my predecessor Pope Paul VI taught, "bear within them the reflection of thousands of years of searching for God, an incomplete quest but one often enough carried out with sincerity and honesty. Theirs is an impressive heritage of profoundly religious texts. They have taught generations how to pray. All are strewn with innumerable 'seeds of the Word'" (Paul VI, Evangelii Nuntiandi, 53).

4. Thus the theme of spirituality constitutes a natural meeting point for the followers of different religious traditions and a fruitful subject for interreligious dialogue. As your Plenary Assembly has shown, the "dialogue of spirituality" is an essential and crowning form of dialogue between men and women of different religious experiences. It enables "persons rooted in their own religious traditions" to share "their spiritual riches, for instance with regard to prayer and contemplation, faith and ways of searching for God or the Absolute" (Ibid., 42). Such exchanges, for which Christians should be adequately trained, can be a source of mutual enrichment and a stimulus to fruitful cooperation for promoting and preserving the highest values and spiritual ideals of humanity. Within this dialogue there will be ample opportunity for Christians to share the very heart of the Gospel message and to communicate "the reasons for the hope that lies within us" (1 Pt. 3:15). Although dialogue can take on other forms – the "dialogue of life", the dialogue of cooperation, and formal dialogue or exchanges among experts – all of which are important, the dialogue of spirituality can contribute a depth and quality which will preserve these from the danger of mere activism.

5. Such a dialogue of spirituality requires a spirituality of dialogue, that is, a vision capable of sustaining the efforts to promote good and harmonious relations between the followers of different religions. Interreligious dialogue is never easy. It requires solid convictions and a great understanding and sensitivity regarding difference. It is

my hope that your meeting will produce the outlines of a spirituality of dialogue which will be useful to pastors and faithful everywhere, for "each member of the faithful and all Christian communities are called to practise dialogue, though not always to the same degree or in the same way" (John Paul II, Redemptoris Missio, 57).

6. As the whole Church prepares for the Jubilee of the Year 2000, we must take into account "the increased interest in dialogue with other religions" as one of the "signs of hope present in the last part of this century" (John Paul II, Tertio Millennio Adveniente, 46). In this context I thank you for your attention to the implications and necessary conditions of this dialogue. It is my earnest prayer that the coming of the Third Millennium will see a deepening and consolidating of ever more cordial relations between the different religious traditions, for the benefit of peace and solidarity among peoples everywhere. Invoking upon you the intercession of Mary, Mother of the Redeemer, I willingly impart to you my Apostolic Blessing.

About the Editors

Ambrogio Bongiovanni teaches at the *Pontifical Gregorian University* in Rome. He is visiting professor at the *Faculty of Theology S. Luigi* in Naples and at the *Urbaniana University.*

He is the founder of *Movimento S. Francesco Saverio* in Italy and has been internationally involved in interreligious relations and studies for many yearsHe worked in India as research scholar at the *Jawaharlal Nehru University* and as associate expert at the *United Nations.*

He is post-graduated in Chemical Engineering (*University of Naples)*, he holds a PhD in interreligious studies at the *Urbaniana* and *Gregorian Universities.* From 2001 to 2012 he was a member of the *Committee for Charitable Interventions in favour of the Third World of the Italian Bishops' Conference* (as expert for Asia). He was visiting professor at *the Pontifical Institute of Arabic and Islamic Studies,* at *Sapienza University of Rome*, and at the *Pontifical Beda College* (of the Catholic Church of Wales and England). He also taught chemistry and carried out research in chemical-physical processes.

He has collaborated with PCDI (*Pontifical Council for Interreligious Dialogue*), WCC (*World Council of Churches*). He is currently co-director of the *series 'Missio Dei', Interreligious and Missiological Studies* of Aracne Publisher, member of the Board of Directors of the *Magis Foundation* of the Jesuits, member of the National Coordination of *Religions for Peace*. He is the author of several publications, including: *Satira e Religioni. L'ironia salverà il mondo?* (2018), (with P. Trianni) *Lanza del Vasto, filosofo, teologo e non-violento cristiano* (2015), *Fondamentalismi* (2010), *Il dialogo interreligioso. Orientamenti per la formazione* (2008), (with L. Fernando et al.) *Interfaith Spirituality. The Power of Confluence* (2014), *Dialogue in a Pluralistic World* (2013), *Windows on Dialogue* (2012).

Leonard Fernando SJ is the Rector of St Joseph's College, Tiruchirappalli, India. For 10 years (2001-2007; 2013-2017) he was the Principal of Vidyajyoti College of Theology, Delhi. He has been a Professor of Church History and Systematic Theology at Vidyajyoti, Delhi and other Colleges in India and in Europe. He did his Master's at Gregorian University, Rome and doctorate studies at Leopold-Franzens University, Innsbruck, Austria. He was the editor of *Indian Church History Review* (1999-2008), editor of *Vidyajyoti Journal of Theological Reflection* (2010-2016) and since 2012 General Editor of *History of Christianity in India,* a series published by the Church History Association of India of which he is the President since 2017. He is the author or editor of 10 books and has published over 100 articles in national and international journals. He is spiritual adviser to Maitrey Xavier Charitable Society since its inception in 2014.

About the Contributors

Anil D'Almeida SJ, is a Faculty member of Vidyajyoti College of Theology, Delhi. He holds a Master's degree in Sanskrit from Karnatak University, Dharwad and a Master's degree in Theology from Vidyajyoti College of Theology, Delhi. Presently he is doing doctoral studies in Comparative Theology at Boston College, USA.

Dechen Dorjee holds a PhD in Tibetan and Buddhist Studies from Central Institute of Higher Tibetan Studies, Varanasi, India. He has 10 years of teaching and research experience in the field of Tibetan Buddhism, Tibetan Language and Tibetan Fine Arts Philosophy. Currently, he serves as an Advisor on the Education Policy Committee to Tibetan Canadian Cultural Center in Toronto, Canada. He is also a professor at LIFE Institute, Ryerson University, Toronto, where he teaches Buddhism & Buddhist Meditation. Simultaneously, he works as an International Language Instructor with Toronto District School Board. Dechen also serves as a Cultural Advisor to Making Room Community Arts based in Parkdale, Toronto.

Shaheena Khatib is lecturer in Physics at Anjuman Junior College, Sadar, Nagpur. She did her Master's degree in Nuclear Physics, B. Ed, M.A Arabic, and Doctorate in Urdu with NET exam with distinction. In addition to her qualifications, she has also studied Bible during her Basic Bible Course. She has a passion for teaching for which she turned down a prestigious post at Bhabha Atomic Research Centre at Trombay, another post at USA.

She regularly lectures on the Holy Qur'ān with special emphasis on the moral and human values of Divine revelation. God gifted sweet voice and style which helps her to penetrate into the heart of listeners.

She has been actively involved for building bridges between different faiths. Imparting positive mind set to Indian youth to make them asset for humanity, women empowerment, inculcating human values in her students. She holds several positions as Director of PEACE FOR PROGRESS, Ladies-Forum, Functional Arabic Classes, Teacher's Credit Co-operative Society Nagpur; Co-Director: IPIL, Nagpur, Course Coordinator on Functional Arabic Certificate Course, RTMNU Nagpur, Arabic Language Certificate Course YCMOU Nashik; Executive Member of Hunger free India Movement Nagpur, All India Progressive Forum Nagpur-Chapter; and Member of Vidarbha Sahitya Sangh, Anjuman Khawateen, Sadar Muslim Library Nagpur.

She has been awarded: Women's Day award, Iqbal award, Merit award by RTM, Nagpur University, Honour Award by Ujjain University, IPIL Nagpur, Saint Palloti High School, Saint Michael Hight School, VSS Nagpur. Her lectures, paper can be found on www.youtube.com, www.explore-Qur'an.com, www.iqramedia.net

Anand Mathew was born in Kerala in an ordinary farming family. He has four brothers and four sisters. At the age of 12, he left home to be a missionary in North India. He had his high school Studies and one year 'Come and See' formation in Alapuzha, Kerala and reached Varanasi on 25 June 1975. Had his further studies in Varanasi, Ranchi, Delhi and Hyderabad. Entered into consecrated life on 29 June 1978. Was ordained a priest in 1987. Worked as a pioneer missionary in Fatehpur mission from 1987 to 1991. Staying in Fatehpur town, he went on bicycle to various villages around the town and far away too, teaching moral science in the Government schools. After two years he started schools for the poor under the trees or in the huts of the poor in six villages. He appealed to the village local self government to take over these as government schools, so that the poorest of the poor can study without paying any fees. In 1991 Fr. Anand was appointed to Vishwa Jyoti Gurukul, the philosophy College cum Seminary of the Indian Missionary Society in Varanasi as the prefect of students. He coordinated the Student's Missionary League. The seminarians visited 24 villages twice a week and educated thousands of illiterate women. Fr. Anand initiated a series of innovative missionary approaches for the future priests such as, street theatre for social awareness, medical teams for identifying TB and Leprosy cases and intercessory prayer groups for the mission.

Seeing his skills in communication, in 1994, he was appointed as assistant in Vishwa Jyoti Communications in Varanasi. From 19995 onwards he has been the director of this centre.

M. Paul Raj SJ, is a catholic priest of the diocese of Sivagangai, Tamil Nadu, India. Born on 15th March 1967, he was ordained a priest on 30th April 1995. After two years of pastoral ministry in his home diocese as Assistant Parish Priest, he worked as a member of the staff at the Tamil Nadu Biblical & Catechetical Centre for four years and went to Innsbruck, Austria. He was a chaplain of a Benedictine nunnery there for eight years and also obtained a doctorate in Biblical Theology from the University of Innsbruck, Austria, with specialization in the Epistles of St Paul. He is at present the Head of the Scripture Department at the Faculty of Theology, JDV, Pune, India and resides in the Papal Seminary and helps out in the formation of the seminarians. He has hitherto published twenty articles on various biblical themes. He may be contacted at maprmay22@gmail.com

Joseph Satyanand joined the Indian Missionary Society in 1963 and was ordained a Priest on 27th October 1974. He holds a B.Th decree from Papal Athenaeum, Poona. He obtained a graduate degree in Sanskrit from Sampurnanand Sanskrit University, Varanasi and completed Master's and Doctoral studies from the University of Poona (in Sanskrit and Indian Philosophy).

He has been teaching Indian Philosophy and Religions from 1976 at Vishwa Jyoti Gurukul, the Major Seminary of the Indian Missionary Society at Christnagar, Varanasi for forty years. Appointed as a visiting professor at some of regional seminaries in the North India, he spent two years in Interreligious Dialogue ministry in Varanasi (1983-85) and served the Indian Missionary Society at Rasulpur in Varanasi Diocese as its Superior for three years (1985-88). In 1988 he became the Dean of Studies at Vishwa Jyoti Gurukul for 4 years (1988-92).

He was elected a General Councillor of the Congregation for a term of six years in 1983 and later, in 1992, appointed as Provincial Superior of the newly created IMS Varanasi Province. In January 1995 he was elected the Superior General of the Congregation, serving the Congregation for two consecutive terms until January 2007.

In 1996 he was appointed a Consultor of the Pontifical Council for Inter religious dialogue for a period of five years. In 2001 he was appointed the Secretary of the Commission for Proclamation of the Conference of the Catholic Bishops of India (CCBI) for a period of 5 years. He also served the Conference of Religious India (CRI) as a member of the Nation Executive for ten years and as the President of the Regional CRI (Agra Region) for five years.

For the last seven years he is living at Matridham Ashram, the cradle of Khrist Bhakta movement.

Books. *Nimbarka. A Pre Sankara Vedantin and His Philosophy*, South Asian Books New Delhi 1997; *Called to Be Divine. Insights into Indian Spirituality,* Media House Publisher, Delhi 2014.

Jerome Sylvester IMS is the Director of Gyan Bharati Theologate at Christ Nagar, Varanasi. He is specialized in Contextual Theology and teaching at different Seminaries and theological colleges. He has published his books on *Hermeneutics of Khristbhakta Movement*, and *The Two parables* a book on biblical hermeneutics which reflect his missionary zeal and creative thinking. He has also developed the *Synopticon Method* for empirical study in contextual theology. He has published a few theological articles and presented papers in various seminars. He is teaching Contextual Research Methodology in Theology known as Synopticon Method at different Seminaries and Theological Colleges and helps research scholars in empirical research in theology. He co-ordinates exposure programme for students of theology from various seminaries. He is a budding theologian and committed missionary with a vision for Indian Church. He was President of the Local CRI, Executive member of Catholic Council of India, he also has been twice Executive member of the Indian Theologians Association. He has become vice provincial for the second time in IMS.

Description on the Cover Picture

"This mural embossment is unique in the history of the world, in the sense that this is the first time a Buddhist monk has ever presented a picture of Christ, in painting, sculpture, or any other art form. This was his first picture of Christ, and with this he began painting a lot of other pictures, some of which were printed in the MISEREOR Lenten calendar [of 2000].

Here he has depicted (his interpretation, of course) the washing of feet by Jesus Christ. He has taken the common meal that the monks are invited to in a home in a normal Buddhist ethos. It's meritorious to give a meal to monks, and the monks normally come with their begging bowls in their hands. It's a sign they are mendicants. They don't have any possessions of their own; they live by begging their food. In Sri Lanka, when they come in procession with their begging bowls for a lunch, a servant of the house normally washes their feet before they enter. And here you see the master of the house washing their feet as they are entering.

The monk is presented through various mudras, dramatic gestures of the hand which are used in normal [classical] drama. The mudra he uses [hand raised, palm facing outward] is "Don't. I won't allow it. This is not done," because the master shouldn't wash the feet of his disciples; the disciple should wash the feet of his master. That's our culture. It's normally the disciples who do all services to the master, not the other way around. Here he has gone against the culture of the place. He is washing the feet.

Then he has put another picture here of two women, one a high class and the other one low class. You can see this from their dress. A person who is familiar with Buddhist temple art can immediately recognize the class difference between the two women.

The other gesture [index and middle finger raised in a "V" shape] means something extraordinarily funny, out of the way, is happening.

This is how, through traditional art forms of the past, the Buddhist monk has brought out the uniqueness of the washing of the feet, even within Christianity, and much more in the Asian culture. It's a revolution.

There is another difference: the rice and water, with the lamp, which means it's a supper. Now Buddhist monks never take supper; they normally take their lunch. In a way, the artist has shown that something Christian is happening, but in a Buddhist way. Mendicants are coming, washing of the feet is there (with a revolutionary change), it is in the night (so it can't be Buddhist monks), and he includes two women. What he brings out is that Jesus is the only founder of a religion who had women in his company, who were not his wife or daughter.

This again shows how a Buddhist sees things that we don't see. This picture presents a new fact: we cannot understand our uniqueness unless the other tells us. It is always by listening to the other that we know who we are. Our identity cannot be presented by us; it has to be detected by the others. This is what is happening here. A Buddhist is telling us, "Your religion has these unique points: the teacher/master washing the feet, women in the company, at the supper, and there is no class difference.

I told the monk, "You have done something without knowing it. You have intuited [what Paul meant when he said], 'There is neither male nor female in Christ' (see Galatians 3:28). Therefore, neither should there be in Christianity." There should not be high caste and low caste, free and slave.

And the third—and this comes out here—in Christ there is neither Christian nor non-Christian (neither Jew nor Gentile). This is a human event. There is no religion here. This is a message to humanity.

I think this monk can grasp the human in Jesus because he belongs to—is the founder of—the Humanistic Association of Monks. He wanted humanism to be the basis of their Buddhist practice. He was fighting against class structure and racial distinction between Tamils and Sinhalese. He belonged to a group of monks who were ready to go to the north and bring justice to the minority.

What we see in Jesus is the attempt of God to teach us how to be human, to be human like God. Here is a picture of Jesus' humanity. Women and men, high caste and low caste, Christians and non-Christians. Everything is erased. His humanity comes out. "Neither in Mount Gerizim nor in Jerusalem," neither Samaritan nor Jew (see John 4:21). In his humanity we will worship God.

For me, this is the most revolutionary picture here. There [in the mural of Jesus listening to the teachers in the temple] we had the humility of God; here we have the humanity of God, which Jesus revealed to us. As the medieval humanist said, "If God could be so human, why can't we be?" Why can't the Church be? Why can't all be? This is the message of Christ.

I think the Buddhist monk as a humanist has captured this better than any artist I know." **Aloysius Pieris SJ:**

Source: http://tulana.org/art-works-at-tulana/